Betsy-Tacy

D0189557

Betsy-Tacy

Maud Hart Lovelace

Illustrated by *Lois Lenski*

HarperTrophy®
An Imprint of HarperCollinsPublishers

Harper Trophy® is a registered trademark
of HarperCollins Publishers.

Betsy-Tacy
Copyright © 1940 by Maud Hart Lovelace
Copyright renewed 1968 by Maud Hart Lovelace
Author note from *Minnesota Writes* and reproduced with permission.
Copyright © 1961 by Instructional Fair • TS Denison
"Maud Hart Lovelace and Her World" (adapted from *The Betsy-Tacy Companion:*
A Biography of Maud Hart Lovelace by Sharla Scannell Whalen)
Copyright © 2000 by HarperCollins Publishers
All rights reserved. Printed in the United States of America. No part of this book may be
used or reproduced in any manner whatsoever without written permission except in the
case of brief quotations embodied in critical articles and reviews. For information address
HarperCollins Children's Books, a division of HarperCollins Publishers, 10 East 53rd
Street, New York, NY, 10022.
www.harpercollinschildrens.com

Library of Congress catalog card number: 40-30965
ISBN 978-0-06-440096-1
First published in hardcover by Thomas Y. Crowell Company in 1940
First Harper Trophy edition, 1979
Revised Harper Trophy edition, 2007
10 11 12 13 LP/RRDH 30

To
BICK and MERIAN

Contents

Author's Note

I cannot remember back to a year in which I did not consider myself to be a writer, and the younger I was the bigger the capital "W." Back in Mankato I wrote stories in notebooks and illustrated them with pictures cut from magazines. When I was ten my father, I hope at not too great expense, had printed a booklet of my earliest rhymes. Soon after I started bombarding the magazines and sold my first story when I was eighteen.

For a long time now I have been happily absorbed in a succession of books for children, chiefly the Betsy-Tacy series. I began these by pure accident. Earlier, for many years, I wrote historical novels and there was a time when I would have told you I was unlikely ever to write anything else. The field delighted me. Especially, I loved the research involved.

I was well into my fourth novel when our daughter Merian was born—quite unexpectedly, because we had been married fourteen years. I finished that novel and wrote two more in collaboration with my husband. But I found myself less and less interested in inventing plots for adult readers. As Merian grew old enough to listen to stories, I loved to tell them to her and I found that most of them centered about my own happy childhood in Mankato. By the time she was seven, and my writer's (now a small "w") conscience was upbraiding me because I had not done a book for several years, I saw suddenly that I could make a book of the stories I was telling her.

The first of the Betsy-Tacy books resulted and ever since then I have written stories for children, most of them about Betsy who is, in some measure, myself. The Ray family is plainly the Hart family. I meet grandfathers now who tell me that they still remember my father's onion sandwiches. It is a great joy to me to have that dear family between book covers.

I must make clear that these are books of fiction. Plots for them have been invented freely. But many— although not all—of the characters are based on real people.

This situation led me into a new kind of research. Letters began to fly. "Tacy," "Tib," "Carney," and other close friends answered lists of questions from me about themselves and our doings when we were young. They drew diagrams of Mankato streets. (Mankato is the Deep Valley of the stories.) They sent old photographs of themselves and their relatives and their houses which Lois Lenski and Vera Neville enjoyed embodying in their delightful pictures. I dived into my own diaries and kodak books and memory books, while the New York Public Library—and later the Claremont libraries—helped out with old newspapers, old fashion magazines, collections of old popular songs, and Sears and Roebuck catalogues.

As our daughter grew up, so did Betsy, and there are now ten mainline Betsy-Tacy stories and three more in which Betsy appears. The letters from children which began with *Betsy-Tacy* flow into our mailbox and are a constant inducement to continue writing juvenile books.

Maud Lovelace

1961

There was a time when meadow, grove, and stream,
The earth, and every common sight,
    To me did seem
Apparell'd in celestial light,
The glory and the freshness of a dream . . .

—WILLIAM WORDSWORTH

1

Betsy Meets Tacy

IT WAS difficult, later, to think of a time when Betsy and Tacy had not been friends. Hill Street came to regard them almost as one person. Betsy's brown braids went with Tacy's red curls, Betsy's plump legs with Tacy's spindly ones, to school and from school, up hill and down, on errands and in play. So that when Tacy had the mumps and Betsy was obliged to make her journeys alone, saucy boys teased her: "Where's the cheese, apple pie?" "Where's your mush, milk?" As though she didn't feel lonesome enough already! And Hill Street knew when Sunday came, even without listening to the rolling bells, for Betsy Ray and Tacy Kelly (whose parents attended different churches), set off down Hill Street separately, looking uncomfortable and strange.

But on this March afternoon, a month before Betsy's fifth birthday, they did not know each other. They had not even seen each other, unless Betsy had glimpsed Tacy, without knowing her for Tacy, among the children of assorted sizes moving into the house across the street. Betsy had been kept in because of bad weather, and all day she had sat with her nose pasted to the pane. It was exciting beyond words to have a family with children moving into that house.

Hill Street was rightfully named. It ran straight up into a green hill and stopped. The name of the town was Deep Valley, and a town named Deep Valley naturally had plenty of hills. Betsy's house, a small yellow cottage, was the last house on her side of Hill Street, and the rambling white house opposite was the last house on that side. So of course it was very important. And it had been empty ever since Betsy could remember.

"I hope whoever moves in will have children," Betsy's mother had said.

"Well, for Pete's sake!" said Betsy's father. "Hill Street is so full of children now that Old Mag has to watch out where she puts her feet down."

"I know," said Betsy's mother. "There are plenty of children for Julia." (Julia was Betsy's sister, eight years old.) "And there are dozens of babies. But there isn't one little girl just Betsy's age. And that's what I'm hoping will come to the house across the street."

That was what Betsy hoped, too. And that was what she had been watching for all day as she sat at the dining room window. She was certain there must be such a little girl. There were girls of almost every size and boys to match, milling about the moving dray and in and out of the house. But she wasn't sure. She hadn't absolutely seen one.

She had watched all day, and now the dining room was getting dark. Julia had stopped practicing her music lesson, and Mrs. Ray had lighted the lamp in the kitchen.

The March snow lay cold and dirty outside the window, but the wind had died down, and the western sky, behind the house opposite, was stained with red.

The furniture had all been carried in, and the dray was gone. A light was shining in the house. Suddenly the front door opened, and a little girl ran out. She wore a hood beneath which long red ringlets spattered out above her coat. Her legs in their long black stockings were thin.

It was Tacy, although Betsy did not know it!

She ran first to the hitching block, and bounced there on her toes a minute, looking up at the sky and all around. Then she ran up the road to the point where it ended on the hill. Some long-gone person had placed a bench there. It commanded the view down Hill Street. The little girl climbed up on this bench and looked intently into the dusk.

"I know just how she feels," thought Betsy with a throb. "This is her new home. She wants to see what it's like." She ran to her mother.

"Mamma!" she cried. "There's the little girl my age. Please let me go out! Just a minute! Please!"

Mrs. Ray was moved by the entreaty. She looked out at the colored sky.

"It does seem to be clearing up," she said. "But you could only stay a minute. Do you want to go to the bother of putting on your things . . ."

"Oh, yes, yes!"

"Overshoes and mittens and everything?"

"Yes, really!"

Betsy flew to the closet, but she could not find her pussy hood. The mittens were twisted on the string inside her coat.

"Mamma! Help me! Please! She'll be gone."

"Help her, Julia," called Betsy's mother, and Julia helped, and at last the pussy hood was tied, and the coat buttoned, and the overshoes buckled, and the mittens pulled on.

Outside the air was fresh and cold. The street lamp had been lighted. It was exciting just to be out at this hour, even without the prospect of meeting the new little girl. But the new little girl still stood on the bench looking down the street.

Betsy ran toward her. She ran on the sidewalk as far as it went. Then she took to the frozen rutty road, and she had almost reached the bench when the little girl saw her.

"Hello!" called Betsy. "What's your name?"

The other child made no answer. She jumped off the bench.

"Don't go!" cried Betsy. "I'm coming."

But the other child without a word began to run. She brushed past Betsy on her headlong flight down the hill. She ran like a frightened rabbit, and Betsy ran in pursuit.

"Wait! Wait!" Betsy panted as she ran. But the new child would not stop. On fleet, black-stockinged legs she ran, faster than Betsy could follow.

"Wait! Wait!" pleaded Betsy but the child did not turn her head. She gained her own lawn, floundered through the snow to her house.

The entrance to her house was through a storm shed. She ran into this and banged the door. The door had a pane of glass in the front, and through that pane she stared fearfully at Betsy.

Betsy stood still, winking back tears, a mittened finger in her mouth. At last she turned and trudged slowly back through the snowy dark to her house.

She had almost reached her porch when the door of the storm shed opened. The new little girl stuck out her head.

"Tacy!" she shouted.

"You needn't call names!" Betsy shouted back. Tacy was shouting her own name, really. But it was such an odd one, Betsy didn't understand.

She trudged on into the house.

The lamp hanging over the dining room table was lighted now. A delicious smell of fried potatoes floated from the kitchen. "Well," her mother called out cheerfully. "Did you get acquainted?"

"What's her name?" asked Julia.

"I don't know. I don't like her. I'm mad at her," said Betsy. It was all she could do not to cry.

That was as near as Betsy and Tacy ever came to

a quarrel. And of course it didn't count. For they weren't friends yet.

They began to be friends next month, in April, at Betsy's birthday party.

2

Betsy's Birthday Party

HE TIME in between was lost because of bad weather. It was filled with snowing and blowing, raining and sleeting. It seemed as though spring never would come. But up in the hills pasque flowers were lifting their purple heads; and down in the valley beside the frozen river, the willow twigs were yellow. Birds were back from the south, shivering red-winged blackbirds and bluebirds and robins. Betsy and Tacy peeped out their windows at them, and if they saw each other they made faces and pulled down the blinds.

However, when it came time to make out the list for Betsy's birthday party, Betsy's mother included Tacy.

"Of course we'll invite the little girl from across the street," she said. And she spoke to Julia. "Will you find out what her name is?"

For Julia, who was eight years old and went to school, was acquainted now with Tacy's older sister. Katie was her name; she was eight, too.

Julia came home next day at noon and said, "Her name is Tacy."

"Tacy!" said Betsy. "Tacy!"

She felt herself growing warm. She knew then for the first time that Tacy hadn't been calling names when she put her head around the storm shed door, but had meant to say that she wanted to be friends after all.

"It's an odd name," said Mrs. Ray. "What does it stand for?"

"Anastacia. She's Anna Anastacia."

So Mrs. Ray wrote out the invitation, inviting Tacy to Betsy's birthday party. She invited Katie, too, to be company for Julia. She invited fifteen boys and girls in all.

"I hope to goodness it will be nice weather," said Betsy's mother. "Then they can play out of doors."

For the Ray house was small. But the sloping lawn was big, with maples and a butternut tree in front of the house, and behind it fruit trees and berry bushes and a garden, and Old Mag's barn, and the shed where the carriage was kept.

It would be much more fun if they could play out of doors, Betsy thought.

She was excited about the party, for she had never had one before. And she was to wear her first silk dress. It was checked tan and pink, with lace around the neck and sleeves. Her mother had promised to take her hair out of braids for the party. She had promised to dress it in curls.

Sure enough, on the night before the party, after Julia and Betsy had had their baths in the tub set out before the kitchen fire, Betsy's hair was rolled up on rags. There were curl-making bumps all over her head. And either because of the bumps or because the party was getting so near, Betsy could hardly sleep at all. She would wake up and think, "There's going to be ice cream!" And then she'd go to sleep again. And then she'd wake up and think, "I wonder if Tacy will come." And so it went, all night long. When she woke up finally it was morning, and the sun was shining so brightly that it had quite dried off the lawn, which had been free of snow for several days.

Betsy flew downstairs to breakfast.

"Dear me," said her father, shaking his head when he saw her. "Betsy can't have a party. She's sick. Look how red her cheeks are! Look at those bumps that have come out on her head."

Betsy's father loved to joke. Of course there were bumps on her head, because the curls hadn't been unwrapped. They weren't unwrapped for hours, not until almost time for the party. Betsy's hair didn't take kindly to curls.

But her hair was good and curly when the rags were removed. It stood out in a soft brown fluff about her face, which was round with very red cheeks and a smile which showed teeth parted in the middle.

"When Betsy is happy," her mother said, "she is happier than anyone else in the world." Then she added, "And she's almost always happy."

She was happy today . . . although she had little shivers inside her for fear that Tacy wouldn't come. The silk dress rustled beautifully over two starched petticoats which were buttoned to a muslin under-waist over woolen underwear. The legs of the underwear were folded tightly under her white party stockings and into the tops of her shoes. They made her legs look even chunkier than they were. She and Julia had hoped that their winter underwear would come off for the party. But their mother had said, "In April? Certainly not!"

At one minute after half-past two, the children started coming. Each one brought a birthday present which he gave to Betsy at the door. Each one said, "Happy birthday!" and Betsy said, "Thank you!" And one little boy who was named Tom said, "Let'th thppeak pietheth." (He meant to say, "Let's speak pieces," but he couldn't, because he had lost two teeth and the new ones weren't in yet.)

Betsy kept waiting for Tacy to come. At last she saw her crossing the street, hanging on to Katie's hand. Tacy held her head down, so that her long red ringlets almost covered her face. You could hardly see what she looked like.

She handed Betsy a package, looking down all the while. The present was a little glass pitcher with a gold painted rim. She wouldn't look up when Betsy thanked her. She wouldn't say, "Happy birthday!"

"She's bashful," Katie explained.

She certainly was bashful. She hung on to Katie's hand as though she were afraid she would be drowned if she let go. She wouldn't join in any of the games. She wouldn't even try to pin the tail on the donkey.

The sun shone warmly so that they could play their games on the lawn. Betsy's mother gave prizes. To please the little boy named Tom she let them all speak pieces. He knew a piece . . . that was why he had been so anxious to have them spoken.

"Twinkle, twinkle, little thtar," he said, his eyes shining like big brown stars.

But all the while Tacy kept her head snuggled against Katie's arm.

At last Julia formed the children in a line. Betsy's mother would play a march on the piano, she explained. Betsy, because she was the birthday child, could choose a partner and lead the line. They would march into the house for their refreshments.

The music started, and when Tacy heard the music she tossed back her curls a little. Betsy was sorry she had made that mistake about saying, "Don't call names!" so she chose Tacy for her partner. And Betsy and Tacy took hold of hands and marched at the head of the line.

They marched around and around the house and in and out of the parlor and the back parlor. Betsy's mother loved to play the piano; she came down hard and joyously on the keys. Every once in a while Tacy would look at Betsy sidewise through her curls. Her bright blue eyes were dancing in her little freckled face, as though to say, "Isn't this fun?" They marched and they marched, and at last they were told to lead the way to the dining room. There the cake was shining with all its five candles, and a dish of ice cream was set out for every child.

Betsy kept hold of Tacy's hand, and they sat down side by side. From that time on, at almost every party, you found Betsy and Tacy side by side.

Betsy was given beautiful presents at that fifth birthday party. Besides the little glass pitcher, she got colored cups and saucers, a small silk handkerchief embroidered with forget-me-nots, pencils and puzzles and balls. But the nicest present she received was not the usual kind of present. It was the present of a friend. It was Tacy.

3
Supper on the Hill

HAT SUMMER they started having picnics. At first the picnics were not real picnics; not the kind you take out in a basket. Betsy's father, serving the plates at the head of the table, would fill Betsy's plate with scrambled eggs and bread and butter and strawberries, or whatever they had for supper. Tacy's father would do the same. Holding the plate in one hand and a glass of milk in the other, each little girl would walk carefully out of her house and down the porch steps and out to the middle of the road. Then they would walk up the hill to that bench where Tacy had stood the first night she came. And there they would eat supper together.

Betsy always liked what she saw on Tacy's plate. In particular she liked the fresh unfrosted cake which Tacy's mother often stirred up for supper for her big family. Tacy knew that Betsy liked that cake, and she always divided her piece. And if baked beans or corn bread or something that Tacy liked lay on Betsy's plate, Betsy divided that too.

While they ate they watched the sun setting behind Tacy's house. Sometimes the west showed clouds like tiny pink feathers; sometimes it showed purple mountains and green lakes; sometimes the clouds were scarlet with gold around the edges. Betsy liked to make up stories, so she made up stories about the sunset. When she couldn't think what to say next, Tacy helped her.

Betsy always put herself and Tacy in the stories. Like this:

One night two little girls named Betsy and Tacy were eating their supper on the hill. The hill was covered with flowers. They smelled sweet and were pink like the sky. The sky was covered with little pink feathers.

"I wish," said Tacy, "that I had a feather for my hat."

"Do you really?" asked Betsy.

"Certainly I do," said Tacy.

"I'll get you one," said Betsy.

She stood up on the bench. They were through eating their suppers and had put their plates down in the grass. Betsy stood up on the bench and reached her hand out for a feather.

Tacy said, "You can't reach that feather. It's way over our house."

Betsy said, "I can so."

She reached and she reached; and the first thing she knew one of the feathers had come near enough for her to touch it. But when she took hold of it, instead of coming down, it began pulling her up.

Tacy saw what was happening, and she took hold of Betsy's feet. She was just in time too. In another minute Betsy would have been gone. Up, up, up they went on the feather into the sky.

They floated over Tacy's house. The smoke was coming out of the chimney where her mother had cooked supper. Far below were Tacy's pump and barn and buggy shed. They looked strange and small.

Betsy and Tacy could see Betsy's house too. They could look all the way down Hill Street. They could see Mr. Williams milking his cow. And Mr. Benson driving home late to supper.

Betsy said, "Wouldn't our fathers and mothers be surprised, if they could look up here and see us sitting on a feather?" For by this time they had climbed up on the feather and were sitting on it side by side. They put their arms around each other so that they wouldn't fall. It was fun sitting up there.

"I wish Julia and Katie could see us," said Tacy. Julia and Katie were like most big sisters. They were bossy. Of course they were eight, but even if they were eight, they weren't so smart. They didn't know how to float off on a feather like Betsy and Tacy were doing.

"We'd better not let anyone see us, though," Betsy decided. "They'd think it was dangerous. They wouldn't let us do it again, and I'd like to do it every night."

"So would I," said Tacy. "Tomorrow night, let's float down over the town and see Front Street where the stores are."

"And the river," said Betsy.

"And the park," said Tacy. "Page Park with the white fence around it and the picnic benches and the swings."

"We may even go there to eat our supper some night," Betsy said. "Let's go some night when your mother has baked cake."

"Do you suppose we could hold on to our plates?" asked Tacy. "When we were riding on this feather?"

"We'd have to hold tight," Betsy said, and they looked down. It made them dizzy to look down, they were so high up.

Tacy began to laugh. "We'd have to be careful not to spill our milk," she said.

"We might spill our milk on Julia and Katie," Betsy cried.

"I wouldn't care if we did."

"It would make them mad, though."

And at the thought of spilling milk on Julia and Katie and making them mad, they laughed so hard that they tipped their feather over. It went over quick like a paper boat, and they started falling, falling, falling. But they didn't fall too fast. It was delicious the way they fell . . . like a swallow sinking down, down, down . . . to the very bench where they had been sitting.

Only now the sunset had dimmed a little and the grass was cold with dew and down in their dooryards Betsy's mother and one or two of Tacy's brothers and sisters were calling, "Betsy!" "Tacy!" "Betsy!" "Tacy!"

Betsy and Tacy looked at each other with shining eyes.

"Don't forget it's a secret," Betsy said, "that we can go floating off whenever we like."

"I won't forget," said Tacy.

"Tomorrow night we'd better bring jackets, if we're going down to Front Street. I felt a little cold sitting up on that feather, didn't you?"

"Yes," said Tacy, wriggling her bare toes. "I wished I was wearing my shoes."

"Betsy!" called Betsy's mother.

"Tacy!" called four or five of Tacy's brothers and sisters.

"We're coming," called Betsy and Tacy, and they picked up their plates and glasses and came slowly down the hill.

That was the kind of picnic they went on at first. Later, when they grew older, they packed their picnics in baskets.

4
The Piano Box

ETSY AND Tacy soon had places which belonged to them. The bench on the hill was the first one. The second one, and the dearest for several years, was the piano box. This was their headquarters, their playhouse, the center of all their games.

It stood behind Betsy's house, for it had brought that same piano on which Julia practiced her music lesson and which Betsy's mother had played for Betsy's party. It was tall enough to hold a piano; so of course it was tall enough to hold Betsy and Tacy. It wasn't so wide as it was tall; they had to squeeze to get in. But by squeezing just a little, they could get in and sit down.

Julia and Katie couldn't come in unless they were invited. This was Betsy's and Tacy's private corner. Betsy's mother was a great believer in people having private corners, and the piano box was plainly meant to belong to Betsy and Tacy, for it fitted them so snugly. They decorated the walls with pictures cut from magazines. Tacy's mother gave them a bit of rug for the floor. They kept their treasures of stones and moss in a shoe box in one corner.

One side of the piano box was open. As Betsy and Tacy sat in their retreat they had a pleasant view. They looked into the back yard maple, through the garden and the little grove of fruit trees, past the barn and buggy shed, up to the Big Hill. This was not the hill where the picnic bench stood. That was the little hill which ended Hill Street. Hill Street ran north and south, but the road which climbed the Big Hill ran east and west. At the top stood a white house, and the sun rose behind it in the morning.

Sitting in their piano box one day, Betsy and Tacy

looked at the Big Hill. Neither of them had ever climbed it. Julia and Katie climbed it whenever they pleased.

"I think," said Betsy, "that it's time we climbed that hill." So they ran and asked their mothers.

Betsy's mother was canning strawberries. "All right," she said. "But be sure to come when I call."

"All right," said Tacy's mother. "But it's almost dinner time."

Betsy and Tacy took hold of hands and started to climb.

The road ran straight to the white house and the deep blue summer sky. The dust of the road was soft to their bare feet. The sun shone warmly on Betsy's braids and on Tacy's bright red curls.

At first they passed only Betsy's house and her

garden and orchard and barn. They had gone that far before. Then they came to a ridge where wild roses bloomed in June. They had gone that far, picking roses. But at last each step took them farther into an unknown country.

The roadside was crowded with mid-summer flowers . . . big white daisies and small fringed daisies, brown-eyed Susans and Queen Anne's lace. On one side of the road, the hill was open. On the other it was fenced, with a wire fence which enclosed a cow pasture. A brindle cow was sleeping under a scrub oak tree.

"Just think!" said Betsy. "We don't even know whose cow pasture that is."

"We don't even know whose cow that is," said Tacy. "Of course it *might* be Mr. Williams' cow."

"Oh, no," said Betsy. "We've come too far for that."

They plodded on again.

The sun seemed warmer and warmer. The dust began to pull at their feet. They turned and looked back. They could look down now on the roofs of their homes, almost as they had done the night they rode the feather.

"We've come a dreadful way," said Tacy. "If we were sitting in our piano box, we could see ourselves up here."

"We would wonder who were those two children climbing the Big Hill."

"Maybe we ought to stop," said Tacy.

"Let's go just a little farther," Betsy said. But in a moment she pointed to a fat thorn apple tree on the unfenced side of the road. "That would be a nice place to stop," she suggested. And they stopped.

Under the thorn apple tree was a deep, soft nest of grass. The two little girls sat down and drew their knees into their arms. They could see farther now than the treetops of Hill Street. They could see the roof of the big red schoolhouse where Julia and Katie went to school.

A squirrel whisked down the tree to look at them. A phoebe sang, "Phoebe! Phoebe!" over and over again. A hornet buzzed in the noonday heat, but did not come too near.

"Let's live up here," Betsy said suddenly.

Tacy started. "You mean all the time?"

"All the time. Sleep here and everything."

"Just you and me?" Tacy asked.

"I think it would be fun," said Betsy. She jumped up and found a broken branch. "This is the front of our house," she said, laying it down.

Tacy brought a second branch and laid it so that the two ends left a space between. "This is our front door," she said.

"This is our parlor," said Betsy. "Where this stone is. Company can sit on the stone."

"And this is our bedroom," said Tacy. "If your mother will let us have her big brown shawl to sleep on, my mother will give us a pillow, I think."

They worked busily, making their house.

"But Betsy," said Tacy after a time. "What will we have to eat?"

Betsy looked thoughtfully about her. "Why, we'll milk the cow," she said.

"Do you think we could?"

"'Course we could. You hold him and I'll milk him."

"All right," said Tacy. "Only not just yet. I'm not hungry yet."

Betsy rolled her eyes upward. "We can have thorn apples too," she said.

"That's right," said Tacy happily. "We can have thorn apple pie."

They started picking thorn apples. But after a

moment Betsy interrupted the task.

"And I like eggs," she said.

Something firm and determined in her tone made Tacy look around hurriedly. Betsy was looking at a hen. It was a red hen with a red glittery breast. It had wandered up the hill from some back yard in Hill Street, perhaps. Or down the hill from the big white house. Betsy and Tacy could not tell. But Betsy was looking at the hen so firmly, there was no mistaking her intention.

"We'll catch that hen," said Betsy, "and keep him in a box. And whenever we get hungry he can lay us an egg."

"That will be fine," said Tacy.

They began to hunt for a box.

With great good fortune they found one. It was broken and old and water-soaked, but it was a box. It would hold a hen.

"Now," said Betsy, "we have to catch him. I'll say, 'Here chickabiddie, chickabiddie! Here chickabiddie, chickabiddie!' like I've heard my Uncle Edward do, and when he comes right up to my hand, you grab him."

"All right," said Tacy.

So Betsy called, "Here chickabiddie, chickabiddie! Here chickabiddie, chickabiddie!" just as she had heard her Uncle Edward do. And she called so well and made such inviting motions with her hand (as though she were scattering feed) that the hen came running toward her. And Tacy swooped down on it with two thin arms and Betsy bundled it up in two plump ones. Somehow, although it flapped and clawed, they got it into the box.

But the hen was very angry. It glared at them with furious little eyes and opened and shut its sharp little beak and made the most horrid, terrifying squawks.

"Lay an egg, chickabiddie! Lay an egg, chickabiddie!" said Betsy over and over.

But the hen didn't lay a single egg.

About this time voices rose from Hill Street.

"Betsy!" "Tacy!" "Betsy!" "Tacy!" One voice added, "Dinner's ready."

"I don't believe he's going to lay an egg," said Tacy.

"Neither do I," said Betsy. "He isn't trained yet."

"Maybe," said Tacy, "our piano box is a nicer place to live after all."

Betsy thought it over. The hen kept making that horrid, squawking sound. Probably there would be strawberry jam for dinner, left over from what went into the jars. And the piano box was a beautiful place.

"Our piano box," she agreed, jumping up, "has a roof for when it rains."

So they ran down the Big Hill.

"We climbed the Big Hill," they shouted joyously to Julia and Katie who had been doing the calling.

"Pooh! We climb it often," Julia and Katie said.

5
The First Day of School

WHEN SEPTEMBER came, Betsy and Tacy started going to school. Julia took Betsy and Katie took Tacy, on the opening day. Betsy's mother came out on the steps of the little yellow house to wave good-by, and Tacy's mother came out on her steps, too, along with Tacy's brother Paul and Bee, the baby, who weren't old enough yet to go to school.

Betsy was beaming all over her round rosy face. Her tightly braided pigtails, with new red ribbons on the ends, stuck out behind her ears. She wore a new plaid dress which her mother had made, and new shoes which felt stiff and queer.

Tacy's mother had brushed the ringlets over her finger 'til they shone. They hung as neat as sausages down Tacy's back. Tacy had a new dress, too; navy blue, it was, because she had red hair. But where Betsy was beaming, Tacy was frowning. She held her head down and dragged from Katie's hand.

She was bashful; that was the trouble. Betsy had almost forgotten how bashful Tacy could be. Tacy wasn't bashful with Betsy any more, but she was very bashful starting to school. "She'll get over it," said Katie, and they set off down Hill Street. The maples were beginning to turn yellow but the air was soft and warm. It smelled of the smoke from Grandpa Williams' bonfire.

"We're going to school, Grandpa Williams," Betsy called to him.

"That's fine," said Grandpa Williams.

Tacy said nothing.

They went down Hill Street to the vacant lot. It was knee deep with goldenrod and asters. It would have been fun to stop and play there, if they hadn't been going to school. But they cut through by a little path and came out on Pleasant Street.

There on the corner on a big green lawn stood a chocolate-colored house. It had porches all around it, a tower on the side, and a pane of colored glass over the front door. It was a beautiful house but they had no time to look at it. They were busy going to school.

They crossed the street and turned the corner and came to a little store.

"That's Mrs. Chubbock's store," Julia explained. "That's where you go to buy gum drops and chocolate men if anyone's given you a penny."

"I wish that someone had given me a penny. Don't you, Tacy?" Betsy asked.

Tacy didn't answer.

Just beyond Mrs. Chubbock's store, they came to the school yard. They came first to the boys' yard, a big sandy yard with one tree. On the other side of the schoolhouse was the girls' yard which looked much the same. But the girls' yard had more trees. The schoolhouse was built of red brick trimmed with yellow stone. A steep flight of steps led up to the door.

At the top of the steps stood a boy, holding a big bell. When he rang that bell, Julia explained, it was time for school to begin.

"Oh, oh!" said Betsy. "I wish that I could be the one to ring the bell. Don't you, Tacy?"

Tacy didn't say a word.

The girls playing in the school yard came crowding around Julia and Katie to see their little sisters. Tacy shook her long red curls over her face. Between the curls her face was as red as a beet. She wouldn't look up.

She didn't look up until the boy at the head of the steps began to ring the bell. Ding, dong, ding, dong, went the bell. Tacy jumped like a scared rabbit and pulled at Katie's hand. She pulled away from the schoolhouse because she didn't want to go in. But

Katie was stronger than Tacy; besides, she was the kind of person who never gave up. So she pulled harder than Tacy and got her to the Baby Room door.

Julia had already taken Betsy to the door, and had said to Miss Dalton, the teacher: "This is my little sister Betsy."

Now Katie said, "This is my little sister Tacy." And she added, "She's very bashful."

"Never mind," said Miss Dalton, smiling brightly. "I'll take care of that. I'll put her right by me." And she placed a little chair beside her desk and put Tacy into that.

Tacy didn't like it. Betsy could tell from the way she scrunched down and hid herself beneath her curls. She liked it less than ever when Betsy was put far away at a regular desk in one of the rows of desks which filled the room. But Miss Dalton was too busy to notice; Julia and Katie went out; the door closed, and school began.

If it hadn't been for Tacy's looking so forlorn, Betsy would have liked school. The windows were hung with chains made from shiny paper. On the blackboard was a calendar for the month of September drawn with colored chalk. And Miss Dalton was pretty; she looked like a canary. But it was hard for Betsy to be happy with Tacy such a picture of woe.

Instead of looking better, Tacy looked worse and worse. She gazed at Betsy with pleading eyes, and her face was screwed up as though she were going to cry.

"She's going to cry," someone whispered in Betsy's ear. It was the little boy named Tom.

"Oh!" cried Betsy. "You've got your teeth." She knew because now he said "s" as well as she did. Besides, she could see them, two brand-new teeth, right in the front of his mouth.

"Yes, I got them young," said Tom.

He sat at the desk behind Betsy's.

Betsy was glad when recess time came. They formed in two lines and marched out of the room and through the front door and down the stairs. The girls skipped off to the playground at the left, the boys to the one at the right. Now, thought Betsy, she would find Tacy and tell her not to be bashful. But when she looked about for Tacy, Tacy was nowhere to be seen.

Betsy ran to the sidewalk and looked down the street. Flying red ringlets and twinkling thin black legs were almost out of sight.

"Stop, Tacy! Stop!" cried Betsy. She ran in pursuit. But it was no use. Tacy could always run faster than Betsy. She ran faster now. At last, however, she slowed down so that Betsy could catch up.

They had reached Mrs. Chubbock's store.

"Tacy!" cried Betsy. "We're not supposed to leave the yard."

"I'm going home," said Tacy. She was crying.

"But you can't. It's not allowed."

Tacy only cried.

She cried harder than Betsy had ever seen her cry. She wrinkled up her little freckled face. Tears ran over her cheeks and dropped into her mouth and spotted the navy blue dress.

Ding, dong, ding, dong, went the schoolhouse bell. It meant that recess time was over.

"Come on, Tacy. We've *got* to go back."

Tacy cried harder than ever.

The lines of marching children vanished into the schoolhouse. A strange calm settled upon the empty yard. From an open window came the sound of children singing.

"We're supposed to be in there," Betsy said. She felt a queer frightened lump inside.

"You go back if you want to," said Tacy between sobs.

"I won't go back without you," said Betsy. She sat down miserably on Mrs. Chubbock's steps.

The door of the little store opened and Mrs. Chubbock came out. She was large and stout, with a small soft mustache. She leaned on a cane when she walked.

"What's this? What's this?" she asked. "Why aren't you in school?"

"We . . . we . . ." said Betsy. Her lip trembled.

"Aren't you supposed to be in school?"

"Yes, we are. But she . . . she's bashful."

"Runaways, eh?" said Mrs. Chubbock.

At the sound of the dread word, Betsy's eyes filled with tears. That was what they were exactly. Runaways. That was a terrible thing to be. How could she go home from school and tell her mamma? Would they ever be allowed to go to school again? Betsy too began to cry.

Once started, Betsy cried as hard as Tacy. Harder, perhaps. And when Tacy heard Betsy cry, she took a fresh start. They held each other tight and wailed.

"Now, now," said Mrs. Chubbock. She limped back

into her store. When she came out, she opened her two hands and each of them held a little chocolate man.

"Do you eat the head first or the legs first?" Mrs. Chubbock asked.

Betsy ate the head first and Tacy ate the legs first. They couldn't very well eat and cry together. So they were eating and not crying when they saw Miss Dalton hurrying across the schoolhouse yard. The sun was shining on her canary-colored hair. She looked pretty but very worried.

"Oh, there you are!" she cried gladly when she saw them. "You weren't supposed to go home, my dears. That was only recess."

The tears began to trickle again.

"I know," said Betsy. "But Tacy doesn't like school. She's bashful."

"And she won't go if I won't," said Tacy.

"No, I won't go if she won't," said Betsy. They lifted anxious faces, smeared with chocolate and tears.

Miss Dalton stooped down and put an arm around each of them. She smiled up at Mrs. Chubbock.

"Tacy," she said. "How would you like to sit with Betsy? Right in the same seat?"

So they went back to school. Tacy sat with Betsy, right in the same seat. They were crowded, but no more so than they were in the piano box. The little boy named Tom sat right behind them.

And after that Tacy liked school.

Betsy had liked it all the time.

6

The Milkman Story

EVERY MORNING Betsy called for Tacy, so that they could walk to school together.

Betsy came to Tacy's house a little early, usually, to be there when Tacy had her hair combed. There was a painful fascination in this business, for Tacy always cried.

Her ringlets were tangled after her night's sleep. When she washed for breakfast, they were merely tied back with a ribbon. Tacy's mother was busy getting breakfast for thirteen, and Tacy's curls took time. After breakfast the time for curls arrived. Tacy began to cry at sight of the comb.

Betsy's eyes grew round and she swayed back and forth as she watched. "But she cried harder than that, the first day of school, Mrs. Kelly."

"Then she must have cried pretty hard that day," Mrs. Kelly would answer. "Keep still, Tacy. I'm trying not to hurt."

Mrs. Kelly was stout and gentle. She was like a large, anxious dove. She was different from Betsy's mother who was slim and red-headed and gay. Betsy's mother knew how to scold as well as to laugh and sing. But Tacy's mother never scolded.

"If I tried to scold eleven I'd be scolding all the time," she explained to Betsy one day.

After the curls were brushed over Tacy's mother's finger, Betsy and Tacy started off to school. They walked to school together, and they walked home together. Back and forth together, every day.

At first it was autumn; there were red and yellow leaves for Betsy and Tacy to scuffle under foot. Then the leaves were brown, then they were blown away; that was in the gray time named November. Then came the exciting first snow, and this was followed by more snow and more. At last the drifts rising beside the sidewalk were higher than their heads.

Betsy and Tacy lay down in the drifts and spread out their arms to make angels. They rolled the snow into balls and had battles with Julia and Katie. They started a snowman in the vacant lot, and added to him day after day until . . . before a thaw came . . . he was as fat as Mrs. Chubbock.

The snow was fun while there was sun to glitter on it from a sky as bright and blue as Tacy's eyes. But after a time the weather grew cold; it was too cold for Betsy and Tacy to play in the snow any more. Their hands inside mittens ached, and their feet inside overshoes grew numb. The wind nipped their faces in their snugly tied hoods; their breath froze on the bright scarves knotted around their necks.

On days like that, as they walked home from school, Betsy told Tacy the milkman story.

It started one day when a milkman passed them on the corner by the chocolate-colored house. His wagon was running on runners; and it wasn't an ordinary wagon; it looked like a little house. The milkman sat covered with buffalo robes, and from deep in shadows came the glimmer of a fire. It might have come from the milkman's pipe, but Betsy and Tacy thought that it came from a little stove inside the milkman's wagon.

That gave Betsy the idea for a story.

The story went differently on different days, but one day it went like this:

Two little girls named Betsy and Tacy were walking home from school. It was very cold.

"I wish we could catch a ride," said Tacy.

And just at that moment a milkman came riding by. He was riding in a wagon which looked like a little house. He had a little stove inside. He said to Betsy and Tacy:

"Hello, little girls. Wouldn't you like a ride in this wagon? I'm through delivering milk, so you can have it for yourselves."

Betsy and Tacy said, "Thank you very much!" And the milkman jumped out, and they jumped in. And the milkman went away.

But before he went away he said, "You don't need to drive that horse. It's a pretty cold day for keeping hold of reins. Just wind the reins around the whip."

So Betsy and Tacy wound the reins around the whip, and they said to the horse, "Take us home, horse." The milkman's horse was a magic horse, but nobody knew it except the milkman and Betsy and Tacy.

The horse started off over the snow. The sleigh-bells jingled on his back, and the wagon ran so smoothly that it hardly joggled Betsy and Tacy. They were sitting beside the little stove in the very inside of the wagon. They were sitting on two little stools beside the stove.

In just a minute they were as warm as toast. It was cozy sitting there with the wagon sliding along. Only by and by Tacy said, "I'm hungry."

And Betsy said, "That's funny. Look what I see!" And she pointed over to a corner of the wagon, and there were two baskets. One was marked, "Betsy," and one was marked, "Tacy." They were covered with little red cloths.

Betsy and Tacy took off these cloths and spread them on their knees, and they looked into their baskets. Each one found a cup of cocoa there. It was hot. It was steaming. And it hadn't spilled a drop. That was because the milkman's wagon was magic like his horse.

And beside each cup of cocoa were doughnuts. They were hot too. They smelled like Mrs. Ray's doughnuts smell when she lifts them out of the lard on a fork. They smelled good. There were plenty of doughnuts for Betsy and plenty for Tacy.

"Isn't this fun?" Tacy said. "Riding along in the milkman's wagon and eating doughnuts?"

Just then the horse turned his head. "Those doughnuts smell good," he said.

"Oh, excuse me," said Betsy and Tacy. "We didn't know that horses ate doughnuts."

"Well, *I* do," said the horse. "Of course I'm a magic horse."

And Betsy and Tacy put three doughnuts on the whip and they held out the whip and the horse opened his mouth and the doughnuts dropped right in.

"Thank you," said the horse. "I'll take you home every day it's cold. I'll meet you where I met you today, on the corner by the chocolate-colored house."

In a minute he turned his head and said, "Of course it's a secret."

"Oh, yes," said Betsy and Tacy. "We understand that."

They had come so far now that they had come to Hill Street Hill. They were halfway up. They put their cups back in the baskets and covered the baskets with the red cloths, and they climbed out of the wagon.

"Thank you, horse," they said.

"You're welcome," said the horse.

They were almost up Hill Street Hill, and they weren't cold at all, hardly, on account of the ride they'd had.

Julia and Katie were just ahead.

"Hurry up!" they called. "Hurry up so you don't get frost bite."

"Frost bite!" said Betsy and Tacy, and they looked at each other and laughed.

"We're warm as toast," said Betsy, stamping her feet.

"We're hardly cold at all," said Tacy, swinging her arms.

Betsy said to Tacy, "Let's go ask your mamma if you can't bring your paper dolls and come over to my house to play."

"Yes, let's," said Tacy. "I hope we meet that milk-man again tomorrow. Don't you, Betsy?"

"Those were good doughnuts," said Betsy. "Maybe my mamma will give us some more."

7
Playing Paper Dolls

QUITE OFTEN, after school, Betsy and Tacy went to Betsy's house and played paper dolls.

Betsy and Tacy liked paper dolls better than real dolls. They wanted real dolls too, of course. The most important thing to see on Christmas morning, poking out of a stocking or sitting under a tree, was a big china doll . . . with yellow curls and a blue silk dress and bonnet, or with black curls and a pink silk dress and bonnet . . . it didn't matter which. But after Christmas they put those dolls away and played with their paper dolls.

They cut the paper dolls from fashion magazines. They could hardly wait for their mothers' magazines to grow old. Mrs. Benson didn't have any children, so she saved her fashion magazines for Betsy and Tacy. And when Miss Meade, the sewing woman, came to Betsy's house, she could be depended upon to leave a magazine or two behind.

The chief trouble Betsy and Tacy had was in finding pictures of men and boys. There had to be father dolls and brother dolls, of course. The tailor shops had men's fashion sheets. But those fashion sheets were hard to get. Tacy's brother George worked next door to a tailor shop. He told Mr. Baumgarten, the tailor, that his little sister Tacy liked those fashion sheets. After that Mr. Baumgarten saved all his fashion sheets for Tacy, and Tacy divided them with Betsy.

The dolls were not only cut from magazines; they lived in magazines. Betsy and Tacy each had a doll family living in a magazine. The servant dolls were kept in a pile between the first two pages; a few pages on was the pile of father dolls; then came the mother dolls, and then the sixteen-year-olds, the ten-year-olds, the eight-year-olds, the five-year-olds, and the babies.

Those were the dolls that Betsy and Tacy played with after school.

Betsy and Tacy stopped in at Tacy's house to get her magazine and eat a cookie. Then they went on to Betsy's house, and when Betsy had kissed her mother and both of them had hung their wraps in the little closet off the back parlor, Betsy brought out the magazine in which her doll family lived.

"Shall we play here beside the stove, Mamma?" she asked.

"Yes, that would be a good place to play," said Mrs. Ray; and it was.

The fire glowed red through the isinglass windows of the big hard coal heater. It shone on the wild horses' heads which ran in a procession around the shining nickel trim. Up on the warming ledge the tea kettle was singing. Underneath the stove, on the square metal plate which protected the green flowered carpet, Lady Jane Grey, the cat, was singing too.

She opened one sleepy eye but she kept on purring as Betsy and Tacy opened their magazines.

"What shall we name the five-year-old today?" Tacy asked Betsy.

The five-year-olds were the most important members of the large doll families. Everything pleasant happened to them. They had all the adventures.

The eight-year-olds lived very dull lives; and they were always given very plain names. They were Jane and Martha, usually, or Hannah and Jemima. Sometimes Betsy and Tacy forgot and called them Julia and Katie. But the five-year-olds had beautiful names. They were Lucille and Evelyn, or Madeline and Millicent.

"We'll be Madeline and Millicent today," Betsy decided.

They played that it was morning. The servant dolls got up first. The servant dolls wore caps with long streamers and dainty ruffled aprons. They didn't look at all like the hired girls of Hill Street. But like hired girls they got up bright and early.

The fathers and mothers got up next. Then came the children beginning with the oldest. The five-year-olds came dancing down to breakfast in the fingers of Betsy and Tacy.

"What are you planning to do today, Madeline?" Betsy's father doll asked his five-year-old.

"I'm going to play with Millicent, Papá." (Madeline and Millicent pronounced papa, papá.)

"And I'm going to play with Jemima," said Betsy's eight-year-old who was named Hannah today.

"No, Hannah!" said her father. "You must stay at home and wash the dishes. But Madeline may go. Wouldn't you like to take the carriage, Madeline? You and Millicent could go for a nice ride. Here is a dollar in case you want some candy."

"Oh, thank you, Papá," said Madeline. She gave him an airy kiss.

Meanwhile Tacy's dolls were talking in much the same way. Both father dolls were sent quickly down to work; the mothers went shopping; the babies were taken out in their carriages by the pretty servant dolls; and the older children were shut in the magazines. Then Betsy and Tacy each took her five-year-old in hand, and the fun of the game began.

First they went to the candy store under the patent rocker. Madeline's dollar bought an enormous quantity of gum drops and candy corn. Next they sat down in their carriage which was made of a shoebox. There were two strings attached, and Betsy and Tacy were the horses. Madeline and Millicent took a beautiful ride.

They climbed the back parlor sofa; that was a mountain.

"Let's have a picnic," said Madeline. So they did. They picnicked on top of a pillow which had the head of a girl embroidered on it.

They swished through the dangling bamboo

curtains which separated the back parlor from the front parlor. And in the front parlor they left their carriage again. They climbed the piano stool; that was a merry-go-round, and of course they had a ride.

After calling on Mrs. Vanderbilt, who lived behind the starched lace curtains at the front parlor window, and Mrs. Astor, who lived under an easel which was draped in purple silk, they slipped by way of the dining room into the back parlor again.

And here they met with their greatest adventure!

The Betsy horse began to rear and snort.

"What's the matter?" asked the Tacy horse.

"A tiger! A tiger!" cried the Betsy horse. She jumped and kicked.

The Tacy horse began to jump and kick too, looking about her for the tiger. Lady Jane Grey was awake and washing her face.

"She's getting ready to

eat us!" cried the Betsy horse, leaping.

"Help!" cried the Tacy horse, leaping too.

They leaped so high that they overturned the carriage. Out went Madeline and Millicent on the highway of the green flowered carpet.

"We're running away!" shouted the Betsy horse.

"Whoa! Whoa!" shouted the Tacy horse.

They ran through the rattling bamboo curtains into the front parlor. There they stopped being horses and raced back, out of breath, to be Madeline and Millicent again.

Lady Jane Grey loved to play with paper. She entered obligingly into the game.

"He's biting me!" shrieked Madeline.

"He's scratching me!" shrieked Millicent.

The tiger growled and pounced.

Madeline and Millicent were rescued just in time. The father dolls rushed up and seized them and jumped into the coal scuttle. Lady Jane Grey jumped in too and jumped out looking black instead of gray, and Betsy and Tacy scrambled in the coal scuttle trying to fish out the father dolls before they got too black. There were never enough father dolls, in spite of Mr. Baumgarten.

Julia and Katie came in just then from skating. The opening door brought in a rush of winter cold and dark.

"Well, for goodness' sake!" they cried. *"For goodness' sake!"* They cried it so loud that Betsy's mother came in from the kitchen, where she was getting supper.

"Betsy!" she cried. "Come straight out here and wash! And use soap and a wash cloth and warm water from the kettle! You too, Tacy."

"Yes, ma'am," said Betsy and Tacy.

When they had washed they put their paper dolls back into the magazines. And Katie helped Tacy into her outside wraps and took her by the hand, and they started home.

Right at the door, Tacy turned around to smile at Betsy. "Whoa!" she said, instead of "Good-by!"

"Giddap!" said Betsy, instead of "Come again!"

"Whoa!" "Giddap!" "Whoa!" "Giddap!" they said over and over.

"Whatever are you two talking about?" said Julia and Katie crossly, which was just what Betsy and Tacy had hoped they would say.

8

Easter Eggs

JULIA AND Katie were nice sometimes. They were nice when it came time to color Easter eggs. That happened a few days before Easter. It seemed to be still winter. There was lots of snow outside, and coal still went rattling into the back parlor stove, but Betsy and Tacy knew that spring was near. All of a sudden they didn't care a bit about sliding down hill on their sleds. All they could think or talk about was coloring Easter eggs.

They colored the eggs in Betsy's kitchen. Tacy's little sister Beatrice was sick. She was Bee, the baby, and she was very sick. Mrs. Ray kept Katie and Tacy over at her house all she could.

Julia and Katie put on big aprons and acted important, but not too important. They let Betsy and Tacy help, coloring the eggs.

First they collected all the cups they could find which had handles missing and cracks along the sides. Then they dissolved the dye in warm water from the kettle, each color in a different cup. The eggs were placed in the cups for a while, and when they were taken out they were red or purple or orange. The colors were so bright . . . it was thrilling to look at them.

On Easter morning everyone ate as many eggs as he could. At Betsy's house, they did.

"I ate three," said Betsy, when Tacy came running over to ask. "And my papa ate five."

"I ate three, too," said Tacy. "And last year my brother George ate ten. But this year nobody paid much attention to eggs at our house, except Katie and Paul and me."

That was because Baby Bee was sick.

They went to church, though, from Tacy's house.

Everyone in the family went, except Tacy's mother who stayed home with Bee. And Tacy had a new hat (navy blue, because she had red hair). It was straw and showed her ears and had stiff gay flowers on the top.

Betsy had a new hat which looked much the same, and she went to church too with her father and mother and Julia. Her mother sang in the choir, and the church smelled of lilies. Betsy liked Easter.

She liked it especially after church, for Katie and Tacy came to dinner. They had chicken, and everyone was very well behaved. After dinner they sat by the back parlor stove and played with their colored eggs.

Katie and Tacy were to stay until they were called for. By and by it grew dark. Mrs. Ray said, wouldn't it be fun if they could stay all night? Katie could sleep with Julia, and Tacy with Betsy. But after supper Mr. Kelly came over.

"Thank you very much," he said. "But Mrs. Kelly wants the children home."

Tacy put her colored eggs into the pocket of her coat. She went home and the next day she didn't come over. She didn't come over the next day, nor the next, for Baby Bee died. Betsy's father and mother went to the funeral.

Betsy was very lonesome for Tacy. The next

morning she went out early before anyone was up. She often went out early in the summer time; Tacy did too. But it was strange going out early at this time of year.

Betsy dressed in all her warm clothes, just as she knew she should. She dressed without waking Julia, and she stole down the stairs without waking her father and mother, and she got her coat and hood and overshoes and mittens out of the back parlor closet and put them on softly and went softly out of the side kitchen door.

The lilac bush stood by that door. It didn't seem to be awake. The snow which had melted yesterday had frozen in the night, and it hadn't come unfrozen yet. Everything in Hill Street seemed to be waiting for the sun. The trees and houses waited in a dim gray light. Behind the white house which stood on the Big Hill, the sky was colored pink.

Betsy walked over to Tacy's house and looked at the upstairs windows.

Tacy must have known that Betsy would come over. After a while she came out of the house. She too had gotten up without waking a soul. She had put on everything warm, the way she knew her mamma would want her to—her coat and hood and overshoes and mittens. She even had her scarf tied around her neck.

She and Betsy looked at each other, and then they started walking.

"What shall we do?" asked Tacy.

"Let's climb a tree," said Betsy.

It wasn't the time of year for climbing trees, but Betsy and Tacy were great tree climbers. So they climbed a tree.

They didn't climb Betsy's backyard maple which was their favorite tree to climb. They went up the Big Hill until they found a tree with branches low enough to reach, and they climbed that and sat there.

Somewhere a bird was singing a little up and down song. They couldn't see him but they could hear him. His busy up and down song was the only sound in the world. Hill Street was still sleeping, but the color in the sky was spreading. Gold sticks in the shape of a fan were sticking up over the hill.

After a while Tacy said, "It smelled like Easter in the church. Bee looked awful pretty. She had candles all around her."

"Did she?" asked Betsy.

"But my mamma felt awful bad," said Tacy.

Betsy said nothing.

"Of course," said Tacy, "you know that Bee has only gone to Heaven."

"Oh, of course," said Betsy.

But Tacy's lip was shaking. That made Betsy feel queer. So she said quickly, "Heaven's awful nice."

"Is it?" asked Tacy, looking toward her. Her eyes were big and full of trouble.

"Yes," said Betsy. "It's like that sunrise. In fact," she added, "that's it. We can't see it during the day, but early in the morning they let us have a peek."

"It's pretty," said Tacy, staring.

"Those gold sticks you see, those are candles," said Betsy. "There's a gold-colored light all the time. And there are harps to play on; they're something like pianos. But you don't need to take any lessons. You just know how to play. Bee's having a good time up there," said Betsy, looking up into the sky.

Tacy looked too. "Can she see us?"

"Of course she can see us. She's looking down right now. And I'll tell you what tickles Bee. She knows all about Heaven, and we don't. She's younger than we are, but she knows something we don't know. Isn't that funny? She's just a baby, and she knows more than we do."

"And more than Julia and Katie do," said Tacy.

"Even more than our fathers and mothers do," said Betsy. "It's funny when you come to think of it."

"She's a long way from home though," said Tacy.

"But she gets all the news," said Betsy. "Do you

know how she gets it? Why, from the birds. They fly up there and tell her how you are and what you're all doing down at your house."

"Do they?" asked Tacy.

And just at that moment, the little up and down song stopped, and there flew past them, going right up the hill, a robin red breast. He was the first robin they had seen that spring, and he was as red as a red Easter egg. He flew up the hill fast, as though he knew where he was going.

"He's going to see Bee, of course," Betsy said. "He'll be back in a minute."

Tacy put her hand in her pocket, and it touched the colored Easter eggs she had brought from Betsy's house.

"Betsy," she said, "do you suppose he'd take one of these Easter eggs to Bee?"

"Of course he would," said Betsy. "The only trouble is how to give it to him."

She looked about her. She looked up, and high up in the tree was a nest. It was a big ragged nest. It looked as though it had been there all winter. But it was a nest; it was a bird's house.

"Give me the egg," she said. "Which one are you sending?"

"The purple one," said Tacy. "It's the prettiest."

"I'll put it in that nest," said Betsy. "The robin

can take it up in his mouth."

So Betsy took the purple egg, and she put it in the pocket of her coat. And she climbed up the tree, higher than she had ever gone before. She didn't look down; she looked up instead. She held on tight with her arms to the rough trunk of the tree, and she felt for the branches with her feet.

She climbed to the very top of the tree, and put the purple egg in the nest.

"There!" she said when she came back to Tacy. "Bee will like that egg."

They scrambled down the tree and skipped down the hill. The sunrise was almost finished. A pale surprised light was spreading over Hill Street. Smoke was coming out of kitchen chimneys here and there.

"Dyeing those Easter eggs was fun," said Tacy.

"Yes," said Betsy, "and I saved the dye. Mamma was going to throw it out, but I teased her, and she let me have it."

"What will we do with it?" asked Tacy.

"I don't know exactly. But something. You'll see."

So they skipped down the Big Hill to breakfast. They were hungry, too. And for once no one was calling "Betsy" and "Tacy." No one was awake to call.

9
The Sand Store

THAT SPRING Betsy's father built a room on their house. He said, "What if our family should grow bigger? There's a bedroom for mother and me, and one for Julia and Betsy. But what about Robert Ray Junior, when he comes along?"

So he hired a mason and a carpenter, and they built another bedroom. It was downstairs, tucked into the corner between the back parlor and the kitchen. It was going to belong to Betsy's father and mother after all. Robert Junior could have one of the upstairs bedrooms, Betsy's father said.

Betsy and Tacy thought it was exciting to have a room built on. They played see-saw on the clean, good-smelling planks. They made curls for their dolls out of the fresh yellow shavings. They dug in the sandpile which the mason had left.

That sand was what started the sand store.

Betsy and Tacy had played store lots of times. The piano box had been first one kind of store and then another, the summer before. It had been a millinery store, full of hats made from maple leaves, and it had been a lemonade store, where they sold lemonade. Now it became a sand store, on account of the fresh new sand.

It happened on the first, good, play-out Saturday in spring. The sun was warm over the earth. Robins and bluebirds and orioles flew in and out of the newly leaved maples, singing as they went. The air smelled sweet from the blooming plum trees in Betsy's father's orchard and the plumy purple lilacs by the side kitchen door. Julia and Katie had gone up on the hill to pick flowers. But Betsy and Tacy had stayed to play in the sand.

The sand was so white and pretty that Betsy got an idea.

"Let's put it in bottles and sell it," she said.

"Where will we get the bottles?" asked Tacy.

"Oh, we'll ask our mammas and Mrs. Benson," said Betsy.

So she and Tacy ran to get the bottles.

Betsy's mother gave them an olive bottle and a pickle bottle and a catsup bottle. And Tacy's mother gave them a pickle bottle and a catsup bottle and a big fat jar. And Mrs. Benson gave them a catsup bottle and a pickle bottle and a perfume bottle with a blue colored stopper. Betsy and Tacy washed all the bottles and took them to the sand pile.

"Now we'll fill them," said Betsy, and they each began on a pickle bottle, putting the sand in with spoons.

Tacy held her bottle up to the sun and looked at it. "I wish that sand was colored like our Easter eggs," she said.

Then Betsy jumped up, and began to jump up and down.

"Tacy!" she cried. "I saved those Easter egg dyes. They're put away in bottles in our piano box."

And sure enough, they were! They were hidden in a corner under a pile of yellow shaving curls, and some Sunday School cards and a box where a turtle had lived. There was green dye and yellow and purple and red and blue.

Betsy and Tacy ran into their houses and got cups (the cups with handles missing and cracks along the sides). They emptied the dye into the cups and put sand into the dye and they left it in the dye until it was colored. Then they spread it out on one of the new planks, each color in a different heap.

While it dried they sang a song which Betsy made up. It went like this:

"Oh, the Easter egg dyes,
The Easter egg dyes,
We could make this sand
Into Easter egg pies.
But we're going to fill beautiful
Bottles instead
With Easter egg yellow
And Easter egg red."

At dinner time Julia and Katie came down from the hill with their hands full of violets and hepaticas, blood roots and Dutchmen's Breeches. They stopped and stared when they saw the colored sand.

"Well, for goodness' sake!" they said. And then they said, "We'll help you fill those bottles after dinner."

Julia and Katie were nice sometimes. Besides it was fun, filling the bottles.

The vanilla bottle and the catsup bottles were

filled with sand of just one color. That was because they were hard to fill; their necks were small. The other bottles had sand in layers . . . purple with yellow, green with red, red with blue.

The jar that Tacy's mother had given them was the prettiest of all. Into that one they had put sand of every color. The mouth of the jar was wide, so that the stripes could be made smooth and even. It made Betsy throb inside to see the shining colors through the glass.

When they had finished, Julia jumped up. "Now I've got to practice my music lesson," she said.

"I've got to take care of Paul," Katie said.

Betsy and Tacy didn't care.

In front of the piano box they put two chunks of wood, the kind that Betsy's mother burned in the kitchen stove. Across those chunks they laid one of the planks from the room Betsy's father had built. They got a cigar box to hold their money, and Tacy sat behind the counter, and Betsy called, "Sand for sale! Sand for sale!" She called it as loud as she could.

At last the children began to come, all the children of Hill Street.

They bought bottles of sand and they paid for them with pins. The bottom of the cigar box was glittery with pins. But Betsy and Tacy wouldn't sell their two best bottles for pins. They wouldn't sell the perfume bottle with the blue colored stopper nor the big fat jar.

"We'll sell them to Mrs. Benson," they said.

So when all the rest of the bottles were gone, they went to Mrs. Benson's house.

She was busy getting supper, but she stopped to admire the bottles.

"What beautiful bottles of sand!" she said. "How much do you ask for them?"

"We don't know," said Betsy and Tacy.

"Would five cents apiece be enough?"

"Five cents apiece!" said Betsy and Tacy. They were astounded.

Mrs. Benson gave them each a nickel, and put the big fat jar on her piano and the perfume bottle on her parlor table.

"Don't they look beautiful!" she said.

Betsy and Tacy thought they did.

Halfway up the hill, Betsy said, "Five cents is a terrible lot of money."

"I know it," Tacy said.

"I'm not sure," said Betsy. "But I *think* that five and five make nine."

"I'm sure they do," said Tacy. "I've heard Katie talking about it."

"It's a lot of money to keep around and not spend," said Betsy.

After a moment Tacy said, "We could go to Mrs. Chubbock's."

"No," said Betsy. "You only need pennies to buy candy. These are *nickels*. We can buy something more important than candy."

She thought and she thought.

"Do you know what I think we'd better buy?" she asked, after she had thought.

"What?" asked Tacy.

"That chocolate-colored house."

"The one we pass when we go to school?" asked Tacy.

"With the tower," said Betsy. "And the pane of colored glass over the door."

"What would we do with it when we got it?" asked Tacy.

"Why, live in it. We'd sleep in the room with the tower."

"We could look through that colored glass whenever we pleased," Tacy said.

So they decided to go and buy the chocolate-colored house.

At the vacant lot they met one of Tacy's brothers. It was George, the one who asked the tailor for fashion sheets for Tacy.

"Aren't you two a long way from home?" he asked.

"We go to school this way every day," Tacy said.

"But this isn't school time. This is supper time," said George. As he spoke the whistle blew for six o'clock.

"Well, it's like this," said Betsy. "Tacy and I earned a lot of money today."

"So you're going to Mrs. Chubbock's."

"No," said Tacy. "We're going to buy a house."

"A house! What house?"

"That house," said Betsy and Tacy, and they pointed through the trees on the vacant lot to the corner of the street beyond. You could see, quite plainly, the tower of the chocolate-colored house.

"How much money have you got?" asked George.

"Nine cents," said Tacy.

"We *think* it's nine cents," said Betsy. They opened their hands and showed him the two nickels.

George pulled his mouth down hard, as though he were thinking.

"It's lots of money, all right," he said. "It isn't quite enough, though, to buy that house. I wouldn't buy it today if I were you. What are we having for supper, Tacy?"

"I don't know," said Tacy. She hung her head in disappointment. Betsy swallowed hard.

"Maybe it's near enough summer," said George,

"so that you two could take your plates up on the hill. Do you remember how you used to do that?"

"Oh, yes!" cried Tacy.

"It was fun," cried Betsy.

They had almost forgotten how they used to eat on the hill.

They looked up Hill Street, and the hill seemed to have been painted with a light green brush. Their little bench was waiting in the rosy sunset light.

"I'll go ask my mamma," said Betsy.

"I'll go ask my mamma, too," said Tacy.

They both started to run.

"And put those nickels in the bank," George called. "Save them! Do you hear?"

But Betsy and Tacy were running too fast to hear.

10

Calling on Mrs. Benson

WHEN SUMMER TIME came Betsy and Tacy didn't need to bother with school any more. They could play all day long. They did play all day long, and they never once ran out of things to do.

"The days aren't long enough for those two," Betsy's mother used to say to Betsy's father.

This was true; although it was strange, for a day was very long.

A day filled all the hours which it took the sun to wheel from behind the white house on the Big Hill, across the vast blue spaces of the sky, to the trees down behind Tacy's barn. By the time evening came and Betsy and Tacy were playing games with the other Hill Street children (not made-up games, but real games, like Pom Pom Pullaway and Run, Sheep, Run), they could hardly remember the cool morning hours when they had had the world to themselves. But in all the long golden time in between, they never ran out of games to play.

One of their favorite games was dressing up. They loved to dress up in grown-up clothes and go calling.

One day Betsy's mother let her dress up in her old tan lace dress. It was a beautiful dress with a big pink rose in the front. Betsy poked an old table cloth underneath her skirts behind to make a bustle like her mother's. And she wore an old hat of her mother's, a round hat with a veil.

Tacy wore a striped blue and green silk dress of her grown-up sister Mary's. Her curls were pinned high, and she wore a big hat covered with flowers. And Mary let her carry her parasol, which was pink with ruffles all around it.

When Tacy was given the parasol, she and Betsy raced back to Betsy's house.

"Mamma," Betsy cried, "Tacy has a parasol. May I carry your parasol?"

"No," said Betsy's mother. "But you may carry my cardcase." She got it out of the bureau drawer. One side was filled with cards which said "Mrs. Robert Ray." A little lace-edged handkerchief, smelling of violet perfume, peeked out of the other side. Betsy's mother carried this case when she went calling. She left a card at every house.

Betsy took the cardcase and Tacy opened the parasol, and they started down Hill Street.

"We'll call on Mrs. Benson," Betsy said.

So they called on Mrs. Benson, and she was very glad to see them.

"Come right in," she said. "How are you, Mrs. Ray? How do you do, Mrs. Kelly?"

She pretended that they were their mothers, instead of Betsy and Tacy. Of course that was the right thing to do.

"Sit right down," she said, and they sat down on the sofa. "It's lovely weather we're having."

"Yes, isn't it?" said Betsy in a very grown-up tone. Tacy didn't talk much; she was bashful.

"I hear you bought some sand, Mrs. Benson," said Betsy in the grown-up tone.

"Yes, I did. Would you like to see it?" asked Mrs. Benson, and she went to her desk and brought out the two bottles full of sand which Betsy and Tacy had colored, the perfume bottle with the blue colored stopper and the big fat jar.

"Mercy, what beautiful sand!" said Betsy.

"Isn't it!" cried Mrs. Benson. "I bought it from two little girls named Betsy and Tacy."

Tacy looked up then, her blue eyes dancing into Mrs. Benson's. "I know those little girls," she said.

"I thought maybe you did," said Mrs. Benson.

After a minute Mrs. Benson asked, "Wouldn't

you like some tea?"

"Tea?" asked Betsy, so surprised that she forgot to talk like her mother.

"Afternoon tea," explained Mrs. Benson. "What ladies drink when they go calling."

"Oh, of course," said Betsy. "I'd love some. Wouldn't you, Tacy?"

So Mrs. Benson gave them some tea . . . cambric tea, she called it, and it was delicious. They had cookies with their tea, and Betsy and Tacy nibbled them daintily. But they ate them to the very last crumb.

When the cookies were gone, Betsy said, "Well,

I'm afraid we'll have to be going. Good-by, Mrs. Benson."

"Good-by, Mrs. Ray," Mrs. Benson said.

"Good-by, Mrs. Benson," said Tacy, not bashful any more.

"Good-by, Mrs. Kelly," said Mrs. Benson. "May I help you open your parasol?"

Then Betsy remembered the cardcase.

"And I must leave you a card," she said. "Here's a card for me and one for Tacy."

Betsy and Tacy went on, down Hill Street Hill.

"Who shall we call on next?" asked Tacy.

"I know," said Betsy. "We'll call at the chocolate-colored house."

So they went on down Hill Street Hill to the corner and through the vacant lot. It was farther than they had ever gone before in grown-up clothes. They held their long skirts high so that the weeds and bushes would not tear them, and they came to the chocolate-colored house.

"Tacy," said Betsy, "I never yet saw anybody around this chocolate-colored house."

"Neither did I," said Tacy.

They looked at it a moment before they climbed to the door.

It sat like a big plump chocolate drop on the big square corner lot. There weren't many trees around it; just a green lawn with flower beds on either side of the white cement walk which led to the porch steps.

Betsy and Tacy walked up that walk and climbed the porch steps.

They rang the bell and waited.

While they were waiting they looked around. The tower jutted right out on the porch. It had windows in it, but all the shades were pulled down. The pane of colored glass over the front door shone ruby red in the sunlight.

No one answered their ring, and Betsy and Tacy rang the bell again. They rang it again and again.

At last the lady next door came out of her house. She looked busy and cross.

"What are you doing on that porch, little girls?" she asked in a sharp voice.

"We're ringing the bell," said Betsy. "We've come to call."

"Tell her about the cardcase," whispered Tacy.

But before Betsy could speak again, the lady said, "Well, the people who live there aren't home. They've gone to Milwaukee."

She went back into her house and shut the door.

"Milwaukee," said Betsy.

"Milwaukee," said Tacy.

They liked the sound of the word.

"I wish I could go to Milwaukee," said Betsy.

"What's it like?" asked Tacy.

"Oh, it's lovely," said Betsy. "Milwaukee. Milwaukee." She said the name over and over.

"While we walk home," she said to Tacy, "I'll make up a poem about it." Betsy liked to make up poems.

"First we must leave a card, though," said Tacy.

"Of course," said Betsy.

They opened the cardcase and took out a card

and put it in the mailbox. Mrs. Robert Ray, it said on the card. They took out another and left that one too. The second one was from Tacy.

While they walked home, Betsy made up the poem about Milwaukee. It went like this:

"There's a place named Milwaukee, Milwaukee,
Milwaukee, Milwauk, MilwaukEE,
There's a place named Milwaukee, Milwaukee,
A beautiful place to be;
I wish I could go to Milwaukee,
With Tacy ahold of my hand,
I wish I could go to Milwaukee,
It sounds like the Beulah Land."

"That's a nice poem," said Tacy. "I like the part about me."

So they sang it together, making up a tune. They sang it all the way through the vacant lot. And just at the edge of the vacant lot they saw Betsy's father who was driving home for supper. He was driving Old Mag and had just slowed down for Hill Street Hill.

"Stop!" "Wait!" "Give us a ride!" cried Betsy and Tacy. They picked up their long skirts and began to run.

"Why, how do you do, Mrs. Vanderbilt?" said

Betsy's father. "And how do you do, Mrs. Astor?"

He stopped Old Mag and cramped the wheel of the buggy, and Betsy and Tacy climbed in.

Betsy took the reins and Tacy held the whip. Julia and Katie were watching from the steps of the Ray house.

"Giddap!" said Betsy.

"Whoa!" said Tacy.

They drove in triumph around the little road which led to Old Mag's barn.

11

The Buggy Shed

BETSY AND Tacy liked to ride home with Betsy's father, or Tacy's. Along about sunset they would walk to the foot of Hill Street Hill and wait. Sometimes they rode up the hill with Mr. Ray and sometimes with Mr. Kelly. Always they rode around to the barn and helped to feed and water the horse, and saw straw put down for his bed and the buggy rolled into the buggy shed.

During the day they liked to play in Betsy's buggy shed. It was dark and smelled of hay and oats from the barn which stood right beside it. When Old Mag was in the barn they could hear her chewing oats and stamping flies, but she wasn't often there. She was gone to the store and so was the buggy. Only the surrey was left in the buggy shed for Betsy and Tacy to play with.

The surrey had two seats and a canopy edged with fringe. There was a pocket in one corner for the whip, and a dust robe to spread on their laps. It was used mostly on Sundays when the family went to church or took a picnic to the river, and on summer evenings when they sometimes went riding while their bedrooms cooled off after the heat of the day.

"Shall we sit in the front seat or the back seat?" asked Tacy now, as she and Betsy climbed in.

"The front seat," said Betsy. For children usually sat in the back seat. So Betsy and Tacy sat in the front seat, and Betsy picked up the whip. Tacy tucked the robe around them, although it was a very warm day.

"Giddap!" said Betsy, cracking the whip.

"Don't go too fast," said Tacy.

"I won't," said Betsy. "I think too much of my horse." That was what her father said, so she knew it was the proper thing to say.

Through the open door of the buggy shed, they could see the Big Hill. It was pleasantly green with an arc of blue above it.

"See things fly past!" said Betsy. "Streets and houses and things."

"Where are we going?" asked Tacy.

"To Milwaukee," said Betsy.

"Goodie!" said Tacy. "That's the place I want most of all to see."

"Well, you're going there now," said Betsy, and she cracked the whip again. "Tuck up good," she said.

"Did we bring a lunch?" asked Tacy.

"Yes," said Betsy. "It's under the seat. There are chicken sandwiches and hard-boiled eggs and potato salad and watermelon and chocolate cake and sweet pickles and sugar cookies and ice cream."

"It ought to be plenty," Tacy said.

They went down Hill Street to Broad Street where the churches and the library and the big houses were; and they turned from Broad Street to Front Street where the stores were. They went past the office where Tacy's father sold sewing machines and past the store where Betsy's father sold shoes.

But they didn't stop.

"We haven't time," said Betsy.

They went on down Front Street to the Big Mill at the end. That Big Mill blew the whistle for six o'clock in the morning and twelve o'clock noon and six o'clock at night. It wasn't blowing any whistles now. Betsy and Tacy rode past it. They rode up Front Street Hill and out of the town of Deep Valley. They were out in the country now.

"I think it's time for our lunch," Tacy said.

"Yes, it is," said Betsy. "We'll stop here beside this lake."

So they stopped beside a lake, and they let Old Mag's check rein down so that she could drink. And Betsy and Tacy sat down in the shade and opened their picnic basket.

"I just love chicken sandwiches," said Betsy.

"This ice cream is good," said Tacy. "It hasn't melted a bit."

"We must be careful not to squirt this water-melon," Betsy said.

"Yes," said Tacy. "We forgot to bring any nap-kins."

When they had finished eating they climbed back into the surrey and they rode and rode and rode.

"I see Milwaukee," Betsy said after a while.

"Do you?" asked Tacy. "Where?"

"See those towers a way, way off?" Betsy said. And when they had come closer, she said, "It looks like the cities on my Sunday School cards, with that wall and all those towers."

"That's right," said Tacy. "I see palm trees."

"The people will wear red and blue night gowns, like they do on the Sunday School cards, most likely," Betsy said.

"Maybe there will be camels," said Tacy.

"Of course there will be camels. I think I see a camel's head now, sticking around. . . ."

There was a head sticking around the side of the buggy shed door. But it didn't belong to a camel. It belonged to the little boy named Tom.

"Hello," he called out doubtfully.

"What are you doing here?" Betsy asked.

"My mother brought me. She came on an errand."

"Oh! Well, you can play with us if you want to."

"What are you playing?"

"We're going on a trip in this surrey."

"Where to?" he asked, coming in.

Betsy hesitated, and Tacy didn't speak either. They liked Tom; but boys were boys; they didn't always understand. And Milwaukee was no ordinary city. Milwaukee was their secret. They had a song about it.

"Just going on a trip," said Betsy. "Is there anywhere you'd like to go?"

"Sure," said Tom. "I'd like to go to St. Paul. I went there once. Stayed at a hotel. And a man gave me a nickel. We went to St. Paul on a train though. Do you think that horse could make it?" he stared at the empty shafts.

"This is a fine horse," said Betsy. "And you may drive because you're company."

So she and Tacy didn't get to Milwaukee that day, after all. But they had a good time in St. Paul. They stayed in St. Paul until Julia and Katie came to tell them that there were lemonade and cookies for the children under the butternut tree.

12

Margaret

THAT SUMMER Julia and Betsy went for a visit to Uncle Edward's farm. They had a good time too. They saw the cows milked and they helped to gather eggs and they played with chicks and ducklings and they rode on the big farm wagons. But at last the time came to go home, and Betsy was glad. She wanted to tell Tacy all about it.

Betsy's father didn't come to get them. Uncle Edward drove them home. They drove into town and up Hill Street and up to the very end of Hill Street. Betsy was looking everywhere for Tacy; she wanted to tell her all about the farm.

But before she could find Tacy she saw her father. He was standing on the porch waving to them.

"Hurry!" he called. "I've got a surprise." And Uncle Edward began to laugh, and stopped the horse. And Julia and Betsy scrambled over the wheel and out of the buggy and ran up the steps of the little yellow cottage, to the porch where their father was waiting.

He was smiling all over his face, and he hugged them and kissed them and said, "Guess what's waiting for you inside the house."

Betsy thought and thought. And she knew they had a cat, so she was going to say, "A dog!" But Julia cried out, "Robert Ray Junior!"

Her father laughed out loud at that, and he gave her a squeeze. "Guess again," he said. And Julia said, "A little sister!" And Betsy's father said, "That's right. A little sister! And we can't very well call a girl Robert, so you and Betsy have to find a name for her. You can name her all by yourselves."

Betsy's father led the way into the house. For some reason he went on tiptoe. And he led the way into the parlor and into the back parlor and into the new downstairs bedroom, and there was Betsy's mother lying in bed. And resting on her arm was a little red-faced baby. A woman wearing a white apron stood beside the bed.

"Julia! Betsy!" cried their mother. "Come here and kiss me, and see your baby sister."

Julia and Betsy tiptoed toward the bed.

The room smelled of medicine, and the woman with the white apron was strange, and Betsy felt strange, too. And she didn't at all like the looks of her baby sister! But her mother was gazing at them with such shining eyes . . . Betsy couldn't bear to hurt her feelings. So she didn't say a word.

Julia actually liked the baby. You could tell that she did. She "Oh-ed" and she "Ah-ed" and she said, "Oh, let me hold her. *May* I hold her, Papa?" And she lifted up one of the tiny hands and cried, "Isn't she darling?"

Betsy was disgusted with Julia. Julia never did have much sense, she thought to herself. When nobody was looking she slipped into the kitchen and out the back kitchen door.

She had thought that the first thing she would do when she got home would be to run over to Tacy's, but she didn't want to go to Tacy's now. She wanted to get away where nobody could see her, and for a very special reason. She went out past the back-yard maple and through the garden and the little orchard and past the buggy shed and into the barn. Old Mag was there munching hay. And Betsy went into a corner of the barn and sat down and began to cry.

She didn't know why she was crying except that everything was so queer. Her mamma in bed, a strange woman around, the room smelling of medicine and that *unnecessary* baby.

"It's a perfectly *unnecessary* baby," Betsy said aloud. "*I'm* the baby." And the more she thought that, the harder she cried, and the farther she scrunched away into a corner of the barn.

Bye and bye Tacy came in. Tacy hadn't seen Betsy go into the barn. She just seemed to know that Betsy was in that barn, as Betsy had known that Tacy would come outdoors early the morning after Baby Bee's funeral. Tacy came in, and she came straight over to the corner where Betsy was sitting, and she sat down beside her and put her arm around her. She held Betsy tight. Betsy went "sniff, sniff," "sniff, sniff," every two sniffs farther apart, until at last she wasn't crying any more. She was just sitting still inside Tacy's arm.

Then Tacy said, "Most everybody has babies, you know."

"Do they?" asked Betsy.

"Yes. Look at our house," said Tacy. "First I was the baby, and then Paul came. And then Paul was the baby, and then Bee came. And then Bee died so now Paul's the baby again. But I expect there'll be another baby most any time.

"You can't keep on being the baby forever," Tacy said, finishing up.

Somehow that made Betsy feel better, to know that Tacy used to be the baby and now wasn't the baby any more. Tacy got along all right. And if this was something that happened to everybody, having a new baby come to the house now and then, why it just had to happen to her.

"Our baby's funny looking," she said in a low voice.

"All babies are at first," said Tacy. "They get pretty after a while."

"My mamma seems to think it's pretty right now," Betsy said.

"Of course," said Tacy. "Mammas always do."

"Julia," said Betsy slowly, "didn't mind at all. She liked the baby right away."

"Well, but she's the oldest," said Tacy. "The oldest is always different."

Betsy rubbed her fists into her eyes to dry them. She leaned back against Tacy's arm and smelled the smell of the barn.

All of a sudden she thought how odd it was that Tacy should be talking like this. Usually she herself did most of the talking. But now Tacy was doing the talking. She was trying to comfort Betsy just as Betsy had comforted her after little Bee died. And she *had* comforted her. All the sore hurt feeling was gone.

"I'll help you wheel that baby out in the carriage," Tacy said. "We'll wheel her to the chocolate-colored house."

Betsy sat up happily. "That will be fun," she said. "And my papa said that Julia and I could name her."

"*Name the baby?*" cried Tacy.

"That's what he said," said Betsy proudly.

"Why, I never named a baby in my life!" said Tacy. "What will you name her?" she asked.

Betsy thought a moment. "Rosy would be a nice name," she said. "Come on, let's find Papa and tell him."

So Betsy and Tacy took hold of hands and skipped down to the house.

Mr. Ray was looking for Betsy. "I was wondering where you had gone to," he said. "Come on in, we've got to name the baby."

"Tacy and I have thought of a name. It's Rosy," Betsy said.

"Rosy!" said Betsy's father. "Rosy! It's certainly a beautiful name."

And later he and Betsy and Julia sat down in the kitchen. They drew their chairs into a circle and talked importantly in whispers. But the baby wasn't named Rosy after all. For Julia wanted to call her Ginivra.

Betsy wouldn't have Ginivra, and Julia wouldn't have Rosy. Julia wouldn't have Rosy Ginivra, and Betsy wouldn't have Ginivra Rosy.

"See here," said Betsy's father. "How about Margaret?"

Betsy liked Margaret better than Rosy. Julia liked Margaret better than Ginivra. They all thought that Margaret was a beautiful name. So they named the baby Margaret.

And Tacy was right about the baby getting pretty. She grew prettier every day.

13

Mrs. Muller Comes to Call

SOON AFTER Baby Margaret was born, two things happened to Betsy and Tacy. The first one was: they climbed the Big Hill, all the way to the white house which stood on the top. The second one was: . . . well, that comes after the first.

It was a late summer day. Goldenrod and asters were coloring the hill. The days were growing short, the birds were gathering in flocks, and there was a feeling in the air that school would be starting soon.

Betsy and Tacy were sitting in the backyard maple, and suddenly Betsy said, "Let's climb the Big Hill, all the way to the top."

"Let's," Tacy said.

So they ran and asked their mothers.

"All right," said Betsy's mother. "But you'd better take a picnic."

"All right," said Tacy's mother. "What a good thing it is that I was just baking a cake!"

So they took along a picnic. And this was the first time that they had taken a picnic in a basket. They packed their picnic in a brown wicker basket, and they both took hold of the handle, and they climbed the Big Hill.

They climbed to the ridge where wild roses grew in June. They had gone that far before. They passed the tree where they had left the egg for Bee in a nest at the very top. They passed the thorn apple tree where they had planned to make a house. There was a pasture on one side, and a cow and a calf were in that pasture; on the other side the country was open and free. They turned to look back, there, but they kept on climbing. They climbed and they climbed, and they came to the top of the hill.

The land was as flat as a plate, and there were oak trees scattered about, and the white house stood there . . . the one the sun came up behind in the morning. They went to the white house and they peeked all around it. They almost expected to find the sun in a pocket behind that house. But there was only a deep ravine, with the sound of water gurgling, and another hill beyond.

"Goodness!" said Betsy. "The world is big."

They had thought they would be satisfied when once they had climbed the Big Hill. But now they wanted to go down in the ravine, and see this water which sounded so merry, and climb the next hill.

"We will some day, too," Betsy said.

But they thought that for one day they had done enough. So they sat down on the rim of the Big Hill and ate their lunch.

They sat on the rim overlooking Hill Street. And they could look down, along the road they had come, into the maples of Hill Street and down on the roofs of their homes. They could see the trees in the vacant lot. They could see the tower of the chocolate-colored house. They could see the red brick schoolhouse where they went to school.

And they could see farther than that for they could see down to Front Street, where Tacy's father had his office and Betsy's father his store. They could see the towering chimneys of the Big Mill where the whistles blew for morning, noon and night. They could see Page Park with the white fence around it. And beyond that, down in the valley, they could see a silver ribbon. They knew that was the river.

"Mercy!" said Tacy. "There are lots of places to go."

They ate their sandwiches and the cake Tacy's mother had made and started down the hill.

And when they reached Betsy's house a great surprise awaited them. Betsy's mother was sitting on the porch, rocking the baby. She was laughing, and she looked very young and pretty, with her red hair (like Tacy's) flying around her face and the baby in her arms.

"You two little rascals, come here!" she said.

Betsy and Tacy came there.

"Do you remember the day I let you take my cardcase?" Betsy's mother asked.

Betsy and Tacy nodded. Of course they remembered.

"Well, what do you mean by leaving my cards at strange houses?"

"Strange houses?" asked Betsy.

"The houses of people we don't know."

As Betsy and Tacy did not answer, she went on: "You must have left a card at that big new house on the corner of Pleasant Street."

"Why, yes," said Betsy. "We did." But she wondered how her mother knew. She and Tacy had kept that visit a secret.

"The people had gone away," Tacy said. But she didn't say where.

"Well, here is what happened," said Mrs. Ray, still laughing. And Julia and Katie, who were standing by the porch, laughed too.

"This afternoon I was sitting here on the porch, and a carriage drove up. A lady got out, and she came up the steps of the porch and said, 'Mrs. Ray? I am Mrs. Muller. It was so kind of you to call.' And then she explained that she and her husband had moved here from Milwaukee. They had bought that house and settled it, she said, and then they had gone back to Milwaukee. But now they have come here to stay and get their little girl in school."

"Their little girl!" cried Betsy and Tacy together. "Is there a little girl?"

"Of course. Didn't I tell you that the little girl was with her? Julia and Katie entertained her, for I couldn't find you two. But she's just about your age."

"What's she like?" asked Betsy and Tacy breathlessly.

"Oh, she's darling," said Julia and Katie. "She's perfectly sweet."

"She has little yellow curls," said Julia. "Short ones. Like this."

"And big blue eyes," said Katie.

"She wore the prettiest dress," said Julia. "White lace with bows of blue ribbon all over."

"And she dances," said Katie. "She danced for us. All by herself."

Betsy and Tacy looked at each other.

"What's her name?" asked Betsy.

"Her name is Tib." "It's short for Thelma." Julia and Katie explained.

Betsy and Tacy didn't say a word. They started down Hill Street. "Do you suppose we'll like her?" they asked . . . but silently. Down in their hearts they thought they wouldn't.

They took hold of hands when they reached the vacant lot. They walked as though they were walking into danger. The tall trees and the bushes and the brush seemed to wait in breathless excitement as Betsy and Tacy approached the chocolate-colored house.

14
Tib

THEY APPROACHED the chocolate-colored house from the rear for it faced on Pleasant Street. On the back lawn was an oak tree which stood on a small knoll. On the knoll they saw what looked like a clothes pin, standing prongs up. It was a little girl standing on her head.

She righted herself when they came near and stood on her bare feet. She was dainty and small.

Her arms, legs and face were tanned, which made her blue eyes look even bluer than they were and her short fluff of yellow hair look very yellow. She stared at them silently out of her round blue eyes.

"What were you doing?" asked Betsy.

"Standing on my head."

"What were you doing that for?"

"I was practicing."

"It must be hard," said Betsy.

"Oh, no, it isn't." The little girl looked surprised.

Tacy didn't say a word. She was bashful.

Betsy stared back at the little girl. It was certainly Tib. "But my sister said you had a white lace dress on," she said at last.

"I took it off when I came home," Tib answered. "I'm not allowed to play in my best dress."

"Neither am I," said Betsy. "Neither is Tacy. I wish we could see your dress, though," she added after a moment.

"Do you?" asked Tib, looking surprised again. "I'll show it to you."

She led the way into the chocolate-colored house.

They went in by the back door. "Wipe your feet," said Tib, pausing on the doormat. The kitchen was so clean . . . it shone like a polished pan. It smelled good, of something baking. A hired girl was standing by the stove.

There was a swinging door which led into the dining room and another door which led into a pantry full of glittery china and glass. The third door led up some narrow stairs and up these they followed Tib.

Upstairs was a long hall with doors admitting to the bedrooms.

Tib took them into one of these, and hanging in a closet was the white lace dress.

"It's a beautiful dress," said Betsy.

Tacy touched one of the pale blue satin bows.

Tib led them down the hall. There were front stairs as well

as back stairs! They went down the front stairs, and just as the steps turned at a little landing, they came in view of the pane of colored glass. The afternoon sunlight, streaming through it, turned it to ruby red.

"Tacy and I like that colored glass," said Betsy.

"What colored glass?" asked Tib.

"That colored glass over your door."

"Do you. Why?" asked Tib. She looked at it as though she had never noticed it before.

"We like your tower too," said Betsy.

"What tower?" asked Tib. "Do you mean the round room? That's our front parlor."

They crossed the hall and entered it.

It was round and beautiful. Hanging over the piano was a picture of an old man giving a little girl a music lesson. The chairs and sofa were covered with blue velvet and there was a bamboo table draped with a blue silk scarf. The table held two little china dolls, a shepherd and a shepherdess.

Tib led them through blue velvet curtains into the back parlor. This had a window seat from which you could see the red brick schoolhouse. A lady sat there sewing. She was short and chunky and had yellow hair like Tib's and earrings in her ears.

"Is this the little Ray girl?" she asked.

"Yes, ma'am," answered Betsy. "I'm Betsy and this is Tacy."

Tacy held her head down and covered her face with her curls.

"Well, I hope you children will all be good friends," Tib's mother said, smiling.

"Mamma," said Tib. "May we have some coffee cake?"

"Yes," said the lady. "Matilda will give you some. But eat it out on the knoll."

So Matilda—she was the hired girl—gave them some coffee cake. It was hot out of the oven. And they sat down to eat it on the knoll.

Tib kept staring at Betsy and Tacy with her round blue eyes. She looked awed and admiring, which was nice but very strange. For Tib was the one who danced, thought Betsy. She was the one who had a white lace dress. She was the one who had a house with front and back stairs and a tower and a pane of colored glass.

Betsy and Tacy looked at each other. Both of them looked surprised. They hadn't expected to like her, but they did.

Tib didn't say a word and neither did Tacy, so at last Betsy said:

"When you came to our house, we were up on the Big Hill."

"Were you?" asked Tib.

"We climbed to the very top," said Betsy.

"Did you?" Tib replied.

"There's a little hill too," said Betsy. "With a bench on it. We eat our supper there."

"All by yourselves?" asked Tib.

"All by ourselves," said Betsy.

"And Betsy makes up stories," said Tacy. It was the first word she had said.

"Do you mean," asked Tib, "that she tells about Cinderella?"

"No, I make them up," said Betsy.

"But how can you?" Tib asked.

"Why, I just do," said Betsy. "Tacy helps me."

"Will you make one up now?" asked Tib.

"Yes, if you want me to. I'll make one up about you and me and Tacy and that pane of colored glass over your door."

Tib was speechless with astonishment, but Tacy jumped to her feet and said:

"Let's go up to our bench. That's the best place for stories."

So she took one of Tib's hands and Betsy took the other. And they walked through the vacant lot and up Hill Street Hill.

As they walked they were very busy talking.

"We've got a piano box we play in," Betsy said.

"And Betsy's got a baby sister," Tacy said.

"We play paper dolls," said Betsy.

"And store," said Tacy.

"We dress up and go calling."

"And Betsy makes up games."

Tib held their hands tightly. She sighed deeply with content.

"I'm glad I came here," she said. "I like this better than Milwaukee."

Betsy and Tacy stopped still. They looked at each other, their eyes as round as Tib's. She liked Hill Street better than Milwaukee! Well, they had always known it was nice.

After a silent moment they went slowly on toward the bench on the hill.

"We'll have lots of fun," said Betsy. "You and me and Tacy. Lots of things will happen."

And so they did.

THE END

Maud Hart Lovelace and Her World

Maud Palmer Hart circa 1906

Collection of Sharla Scannell Whalen

MAUD HART LOVELACE was born on April 25, 1892, in Mankato, Minnesota. Like Betsy, Maud followed her mother around the house at age five asking questions such as "How do you spell 'going down the street'?" for the stories she had already begun to write. Soon she was writing poems and plays. When Maud was ten, a booklet of her poems was printed; and by age eighteen, she had sold her first short story.

The Hart family left Mankato shortly after Maud's high school graduation in 1910 and settled in Minneapolis, where Maud attended the University of Minnesota. In 1917, she married Delos W. Lovelace, a newspaper reporter who later became a popular writer of short stories.

The Lovelaces' daughter, Merian, was born in 1931. Maud would tell her daughter bedtime stories about her childhood, and it was these stories that gave her the idea of writing the Betsy-Tacy books. Maud did not intend to write an entire series when *Betsy-Tacy*, the first book, was published in 1940, but readers asked for more stories. So Maud took Betsy through high school and beyond college to the "great world" and marriage. The final book in the series, *Betsy's Wedding*, was published in 1955.

The Betsy-Tacy books are based very closely on Maud's own life. "I could make it all up, but in these Betsy-Tacy stories, I love to work from real incidents," Maud wrote. "The Ray family is a true portrayal of the Hart family. Mr. Ray is like Tom Hart; Mrs. Ray like Stella Palmer Hart; Julia like Kathleen; Margaret like Helen; and Betsy is like me, except that, of course, I glamorized her to make her a proper heroine." Tacy and Tib are based on Maud's real-life best friends, Frances "Bick" Kenney and Marjorie "Midge" Gerlach, and Deep Valley is based on Mankato.

In fact, so much in the books was taken from real life that it is sometimes difficult to draw the line between fact and fiction. And through the years, Maud received a great deal of fan mail from readers who were fascinated by the question—what is true, and what is made up?

About Betsy-Tacy

IN THE SPRING OF 1897, Maud Hart and Frances "Bick" Kenney met at Maud's fifth birthday party and became lifelong friends—just like Betsy and Tacy. As Maud wrote to Bick Kenney's granddaughter in 1960, when she was sixty-eight years old, "Tacy certainly is your red-haired grandmother and has been my dearest friend ever since my fifth birthday."

In the story, Betsy thinks Tacy is calling names when she first introduces herself because her name is so unusual. (Maud first discovered the name "Tacy" in a colonial newspaper when she was doing research for another book.) We don't know if this happened in real life, but it's possible that a similar misunderstanding resulted when Bick told Maud *her* name, which is also a bit unusual. Bick Kenney's niece explained the origin of the nickname: "Frances Kenney had very red hair as a child and was called 'Brick.' Not being old enough to pronounce it properly, she called herself 'Bick.'" And Bick is the name she used throughout her life.

Maud seemed to recall the occasion of her fifth birthday very vividly, and much of the description

Maud's straight hair was curled for these photographs, taken for the occasion of her fifth birthday.

All three portraits from the collection of Susan Ryder

Lois Lenski probably referred to the photos when she drew Betsy in her special party dress.

of the party in the book was based on her memories. For example, she remembered that she wore a "checked silk [dress] in tan, rose, and cream," like Betsy's. And Bick really did bring Maud a little glass pitcher as a birthday gift. Although its gold-painted rim has now worn away, the pitcher can be seen today in the Maud Hart Lovelace wing of the Minnesota Valley Regional Library in Mankato, Minnesota.

In fact, Betsy and Tacy's adventures throughout the book are based on Maud's real childhood experiences. In an interview, Maud described some of the games she and Bick used to play, which will sound very familiar: "We used to color sand and put it in bottles and have sand stores and sell it. We cut our paper dolls out of the magazines. We dressed up in our mothers' long skirts. We went on picnics."

In 1897, there really was a bench on the hill at the top of the street where Maud and Bick ate their suppers, although it was gone by 1906 or 1907. But readers may be pleased to know that a memorial bench was placed there in 1989, and it is still there today—a testimony to the powerful effect of Maud's writing, and in commemoration of a very special friendship.

Maud (right) and Bick (left) were lifelong friends— here they are at age ten.

Maud Hart Lovelace Archive

Collection of Sharla Scannell Whalen

The glass pitcher that Bick gave to Maud for her fifth birthday is now on display at the public library in Mankato.

Collection of Sharla Scannell Whalen

Maud lived with her family in this little house at 333 Center Street.

The Ray house, at 333 Hill Street, closely resembles Maud's.

Maud's mother, Stella Palmer Hart, was a schoolteacher before her marriage to Tom Hart.

Maud Hart Lovelace Archive

Maud Hart Lovelace Archive

In this photo, Kathleen Hart, Maud's older sister and the model for Julia Ray, is about eight years old.

Blue Earth County Historical Society

*Maud and her friends attended Pleasant Grove School,
a redbrick building that was built in 1871.*

Lois Lenski's drawing of the school-house.

Maud once spoke of "the fresh exciting world in which children live" and said, "I do think I remember that better than most grown-ups." Many generations of Betsy-Tacy fans would certainly agree!

Maud Hart Lovelace died on March 11, 1980. But her legacy lives on in the beloved series she created and in her legions of fans, many of whom are members of the Betsy-Tacy Society and the Maud Hart Lovelace Society. For more information, write to:

The Betsy-Tacy Society
P.O. Box 94
Mankato, MN 56002-0094
(507) 345-9777
www.betsy-tacysociety.org

The Maud Hart Lovelace Society
Fifty 94th Circle NW, # 201
Minneapolis, MN 55448

Adapted from *The Betsy-Tacy Companion: A Biography of Maud Hart Lovelace* by Sharla Scannell Whalen

This map of the Hill Street neighborhood by Lois Lenski was printed on the endpapers of early editions of the first four Betsy-Tacy books.

The other Little Bear, or maybe it was the fellow Hugh
was talking to, the Grizzly — I can't recall which — said,
"That's funny."

Books by Ken Blanchard

THE ONE MINUTE MANAGER BUILDS HIGH PERFORMING TEAMS
(with Don Carew and Eunice Parisi-Carew), 1990

THE ONE MINUTE MANAGER MEETS THE MONKEY
(with William Oncken, Jr. and Hal Burrows), 1989

MANAGEMENT OF ORGANIZATIONAL BEHAVIOR;
UTILIZING HUMAN RESOURCES
(with Paul Hersey), 5th edition, 1988

THE POWER OF ETHICAL MANAGEMENT
(with Norman Vincent Peale), 1988

THE ONE MINUTE MANAGER GETS FIT
(with D. W. Edington and Marjorie Blanchard), 1986

LEADERSHIP AND THE ONE MINUTE MANAGER
(with Patricia Zigarmi and Drea Zigarmi), 1985

ORGANIZATIONAL CHANGE THROUGH EFFECTIVE LEADERSHIP
(with Robert H. Guest and Paul Hersey), 2nd edition, 1985

PUTTING THE ONE MINUTE MANAGER TO WORK
(with Robert Lorber), 1984

THE ONE MINUTE MANAGER
(with Spencer Johnson), 1982

THE FAMILY GAME:
A SITUATIONAL APPROACH TO EFFECTIVE PARENTING
(with Paul Hersey), 1979

Playing the
Great Game of
GOLF

Playing the Great Game of

GOLF

Making Every Minute Count

Ken Blanchard

co-author of *The One Minute Manager*®
president of The Golf University

Foreword by
Bob Toski

Afterword by
Chuck Hogan

WILLIAM MORROW AND COMPANY, INC.

NEW YORK

Copyright © 1992 by Blanchard Family Partnership

All rights reserved. No part of this book may be reproduced or utilized in any form or by any means, electronic or mechanical, including photocopying, recording, or by any information storage or retrieval system, without permission in writing from the Publisher. Inquiries should be addressed to Permissions Department, William Morrow and Company, Inc., 1350 Avenue of the Americas, New York, NY 10019.

It is the policy of William Morrow and Company, Inc., and its imprints and affiliates, recognizing the importance of preserving what has been written, to print the books we publish on acid-free paper, and we exert our best efforts to that end.

Library of Congress Cataloging-in-Publication Data

Blanchard, Kenneth M.
   Playing the great game of golf : making every *minute* count / Ken Blanchard.
       p.   cm.
     ISBN 0-688-12125-X
     1. Golf.   I. Title.
   GV965.B558   1992
   796.352—dc20   92-15319
                                                                                 CIP

Printed in the United States of America

3 4 5 6 7 8 9 10

*To Anyone Who
Has Ever Played the
Great Game of Golf*

Foreword

When Jerry Tarde, editor of *Golf Digest*, called me in the fall of 1984 to ask if I would consider writing an article entitled "The One Minute Golfer" with the co-author of the best-selling book *The One Minute Manager®* I was amused and fascinated. My amusement came from the suggested title of the article. Now, I know this is the age of instant everything, but a "One Minute Golfer" might be taking this a little too far.

My fascination came from my lifelong desire to learn. When I stop learning, I figure, I might as well lie down—because it's all over. So I was open to see what I could learn about the teaching of golf from a Ph.D. business professor and management consultant.

I liked Ken Blanchard the moment I met him. He has a spark and a twinkle in his eye that immediately invites an exchange of ideas. Rather than a stuffy college professor, I found another lifelong learner. I found that the way he was teaching executives about managing people was exactly the way I taught my golf students. His One Minute Goal Setting philosophy (that all good performance starts with clear goals) was right on. Once I have told my students what I think it will take for them to improve, then Ken's One Minute Praising and One Minute Reprimands come into play. I love to acknowledge and praise my students when they are learning and showing progress; and I have never shied away from reprimanding more experienced players if they are getting careless and not using the skills they have already developed. My desire to help my students play better is so strong that I am willing to do whatever it takes to develop their skills or get them back on track. I found the One Minute Management philosophy a good way to describe some of the ways I teach.

I also realized that One Minute Management highlights my hope for all my students: that they will learn enough about golf and the golf swing to be able to set realistic goals for their own game as well as praise and reprimand their own performance when appropriate. So I enjoyed co-authoring "The One Minute Golfer" article with Ken Blanchard. I am also delighted, in retrospect, that our time together marked the beginning of his thinking about the teaching and the learning of golf, because I feel he is making a real contribution to the game.

When Ken sent me a draft copy of *Playing the Great Game of Golf*, I was thrilled to learn how far his thinking about golf has come since we first met. I don't believe there is any other golf book quite like this one. Beginning with an insightful chapter entitled "Purpose: Why Do You Play Golf?" and ending with "Commitment: What Can You Do to Follow Through on Your Good Intentions?," Ken leads a self-management journey that should help every player—from a beginner to a low handicapper—enjoy golf more and accomplish the results he or she desires.

Written in an informal storytelling style, *Playing the Great Game of Golf* is crammed full of wisdom. I know Ken Blanchard's thinking will help you make every *minute* you spend on golf *count*. Enjoy this book and count your blessings.

—Bob Toski

Contents

Introduction

My hope in writing this book is to help you enjoy the great game of golf more and achieve the results you desire. You may ask: Why is a management writer and consultant qualified to write a book on golf? After all, I'm not a pro or even a golfer who shoots in the 70's. I'm just a lover of the game. As someone once said, "Life is what happens to you when you are planning to do something else." Let me explain.

In the fall of 1984, I got a call from Jerry Tarde, the editor of *Golf Digest*. He had just finished reading Spencer Johnson's and my best-selling book *The One Minute Manager*. In that book, the main character, who got good results without taking much time, commented about the problems associated with unclear goals:

> *It's like playing golf at night. A lot of my friends have given up golf and when I asked them why, they said, "Because the courses are too crowded." When I suggested that they play at night, they laughed because who would ever play golf without being able to see the pins.*[1]

Jerry and his staff enjoyed that reference to golf and wondered if I played the game.

"Yes," I said, "I've been a fanatic for years."

Jerry then asked if I would be willing to write an article with one of *Golf Digest*'s top instructors entitled "The One Minute Golfer," applying to golf the three secrets of the One Minute Manager: Goal Setting, Praising, and Reprimanding.

"That sounds like a fun idea," I said. "I'd be happy to do it if I could write it with Bob Toski." I had heard a lot about Toski. Golf and Toski were synonymous. He was a great tour player, master teacher, and widely read author. And besides, I had heard he was a real character. No one ever forgets an experience with Bob Toski.

Jerry Tarde agreed we'd be a dynamic duo, so I flew to Florida to meet Toski. Bob and I really hit it off well. After one day together and a couple of phone calls, "The One Minute Golfer" was launched and wound up as the cover story for the June 1985 issue of *Golf Digest*. The story used the *One Minute Manager*® parable format while attempting to show how the three secrets of One Minute Management apply to self-management and the mental aspect of golf: One Minute Goal Setting (the importance of setting and visualizing clear goals), One Minute Praising (praising yourself for doing something right), and One Minute Reprimands (redirecting yourself when things go wrong without dwelling on your mistakes).

The work I did with Toski was the beginning of my efforts to apply what I have been sharing with managers for years to the playing of golf. When the response to that article was positive, I was invited to attend a five-day VIP *Golf Digest* School in Tuscaloosa, Alabama, with Toski and other top *Golf Digest* teachers, including John Elliott, Hank Johnson, Davis Love, and Bob Ness. I jumped at the opportunity and it proved to be a wonderful time. Although Dr. Bob Rotella, a sports psychologist, did a short session on the mental aspect of the game, the emphasis in the *Golf Digest* School was on the mechanical aspects of the game: full swing, pitching, chipping, sand play, and putting.

My experience writing the article with Toski and attending the *Golf Digest* School piqued my interest in the teaching of golf. To learn more about the mental side of the game, I decided to attend a three-day golf school conducted by Chuck Hogan, founder of Sports Enhancement Associates (S.E.A.) and the mental coach for such top-flight PGA and LPGA players as Raymond Floyd, Peter Jacobsen, Johnny Miller, Cindy Rarick, Mike Reid, Colleen Walker, and Mary Beth Zimmerman. Chuck is the author of the book *Five Days to Golfing Excellence* and the best-selling video *NICE SHOT!*

Chuck's philosophy is that there is *always* a better golfer inside struggling to get out! The trouble is, most of us try to learn and remember *too many things* when we play. Swing! Grip! Alignment! Balance! Distance! The mind boggles, the brain rebels, and the shot whistles off into the rough. Chuck feels that there are some key mechanics that every golfer should know, but he places the main emphasis on the relationship between mind and body and on making golf fun and learning easy. What I started to realize was that golf is more than just swinging a club—it is a mental game too. Spending time with Chuck Hogan added a whole new dimension to what I knew about golf and learning.

It became clear to me that golf was a unique blend of mechanical skill and mental acuity—and neither one was more important than the other. Norman Vincent Peale emphasized the balance of mechanical and mental skills when we were working together on our book, *The Power of Ethical Management*. Dr. Peale said that some people who read his classic book, *The Power of Positive Thinking*, came away believing that all you had to do to be successful in life was to be a positive thinker. What they overlooked was his continual advice that, besides positive thinking, you also need some skills. This is nicely illustrated in the story of the golfer who went to his bag and got an old ball out as he approached the tee on a water hole. When he had teed up this old ball, there was a flash of lightning in the sky and a booming voice shouted down: "Use a new ball! Be a positive thinker!"

Hearing that authoritative command, the golfer went back to his bag and took out a brand-new ball. After he teed up this new ball, our golfer stepped aside and took a practice swing. Immediately there was another flash of lightning in the sky. This time the booming voice shouted: "Use an old ball!"

After recognizing these two important aspects of golf—mechanical and mental—I got excited about helping to create a golf school that combined "the best" that is known about these aspects of golf with "the best" that is known from my field—the behavioral sciences—about coaching, self-management, and changing or improving performance. My particular concern was that students should *play better immediately* and enjoy golf more after attending the school. The Golf University at San Diego, California, which I helped found in 1988 and is now headquartered at the Rancho Bernardo Inn, is, to the best of my knowledge, the only golf school in the world that teaches this integration.

Shortly after starting the Golf University, we realized that there were *two other components* of golf effectiveness—the *physical* side and *club fitting*—that had to be included in the curriculum. I had become involved in the physical side of sports when writing *The One Minute Manager Gets Fit* with Dr. D. W. Edington, head of the Fitness Research Center at the University of Michigan, Ann Arbor, and my wife, Margie, an expert on health promotion and life planning. What is the difference between the mechanical and the physical sides of golf? The mechanical side is about skills; the physical side has to do with the physical *you*—your flexibility, strength, and endurance. Good golfers are in good shape. For example, when I first met Bob Toski, he told me the best way I could improve my golf game was to lose forty pounds. He felt that alone could help my flexibility, strength, and endurance. He was right. I also learned in working with Pete Egosque, the sports functionalist who helped Jack Nicklaus control his back problems, that I could improve more by doing daily flexibility exercises than by standing on the range hitting balls. It's tough when you realize you have to get in shape to play golf, not play golf to get in shape.

I first learned about club fitting from a representative with Henry Griffiths, a pioneer company in the custom-fitted golf club business in the United States, and later learned much more about it from a gentleman with a delightful English accent, John Tudor, founder of Pro Golf Worldwide, headquartered in England. Pro Golf Worldwide is the longest-established custom-fitting center in the world, and its experts are acknowledged as the leading authorities on golf shafts. I soon realized that with the clubs I was using, even if I made an excellent swing in good athletic balance, the ball would fly to the right of the target. I had developed some bad habits in trying to compensate for my clubs. This was mind-blowing to me because I always believed the kind of clubs you used didn't matter as long as they were a name brand.

As a result of learning about the physical and club-fitting aspects of golf, it became important that all of our Golf University programs, besides emphasizing the mechanical and mental skills, included an exercise program and an opportunity for students to have their clubs properly fitted.

How This Book Is Organized

While the Golf University curriculum integrates these four aspects of golf, this book will emphasize only one. It will show how the same skills used by winning business managers can be applied to the self-management and mental aspects of your own golf game and result in lower scores and more enjoyment.

Playing the Great Game of Golf will not try to change your grip, turn, or swing. And it doesn't include any information on the physical or club-fitting aspects of the game. Instead you'll learn: how to be clear on why you play golf; how to set goals and attain them; how to shed bad habits; how to become your own coach; how to take out on the course what you've learned; and how to stay committed to your good intentions. The material is not theoretical. It has been tested with our Golf University students on the range and in actual play. I guarantee that it will help you enjoy golf more, improve your game, and make every minute you spend on golf count!

Part One, GOLF AND YOU, begins with a chapter called "Purpose: Why Do You Play Golf?" Here we discuss an important question all golfers should answer, "Why am I playing this game?" If you take the time to ponder and answer this question, you will have a home base to go back to when you get discouraged about your game or when the "wheels come off" during a round. Knowing clearly why you play golf will help you have much more fun and be better positioned to achieve the results you desire. Then and only then can we counter Mark Twain's definition of golf as "a walk ruined."

Part One then moves to "Goal Setting: What Do You Want to Accomplish?" Once you know why you play golf, then you are ready to set some enjoyment and performance goals. This is important because all good performance starts with clear goals. This chapter will help you set long-term goals (six months), short-term goals (this round), immediate goals (this shot), and practice goals (things you want to improve). Since this book is intended to improve your enjoyment and performance, suggestions will also be made on how to monitor your practice as well as on-course behavior that might divert you from goal accomplishment.

Part Two, GETTING BETTER AT GOLF, begins by bringing reality to the concept of change and improvement. "Change: Why Is It Difficult to Learn New Habits?" discusses seven important aspects of change that you need to know to learn to play better golf. This information will help you overcome any resistance to change you might have. After all, learning takes place only when a change in attitude or behavior/performance has occurred. And this book is all about learning and improving your performance.

Part Two ends with a chapter on "Instruction: How Do You Become Your Own Coach?" This chapter integrates the three secrets of the One Minute Manager with leadership concepts I have been teaching for years, and it shows you the importance of moving from dependency as a learner to independence as a player. This understanding is essential if you ever hope to manage your own journey to better golf.

Part Three, MAINTAINING YOUR PROGRESS, starts with "Application: How Do You Use What You've Learned?" This chapter gives specific strategies for implementing on the golf course new things that you have learned about your golf game. The important thing about learning something new is not what happens while you are learning it, but what happens when you have finished and are out on the golf course applying what you have learned.

This book closes with "Commitment: What Can You Do to Follow Through on Your Good Intentions?" This chapter provides a concise review of the key concepts in the book and shows you how to personalize each concept and apply it to your own game. It ends with an important distinction between commitment and interest. This concluding chapter puts all the power for improving your golf game back in your hands, but gives you some clear-cut suggestions to help permanent improvement happen.

I hope this book helps you enjoy golf more and achieve the results you desire. Good luck!

—Ken Blanchard

Playing the
Great Game of
GOLF

PART ONE
GOLF AND YOU

CHAPTER 1
Purpose: Why Do You Play Golf?

Golf is a non-violent game played violently from within.
—Bob Toski

When I first heard Bob Toski talk about golf as a "non-violent game played violently from within," I smiled because it hit home with me. I've always been amazed how seriously some people take the game and, in the process, make themselves and others miserable on the golf course. They get frustrated and angry with themselves and sometimes even end up throwing clubs, ranting and raving, and generally ruining everyone's time. They create violence within. They never seem to be playing well enough.

While I am determined to improve my playing and set goals like winning the Senior Championship at my club, I am even more committed to appreciating and enjoying the moment-to-moment experience of this great game of golf. How I score on any given hole or any particular day is only one part of the total experience. And yet, when you observe some people on the golf course, you would think that what they score is the *only* part of the game that is important to them.

Patty Berg, one of the greatest golfers of all time and a lifelong heroine of mine, told a wonderful story at the 1990 Women in Golf Summit in Orlando, Florida, that makes a joke of some people's ultimate obsession with their score. According to her, a golfer hit his drive into a fairway bunker. He chose a 5-iron to try to get the ball out of the trap and advance it toward the green. When he hit the shot, he pulled it and the ball struck a tree.

The ball ricocheted off the tree and hit the man in the head, killing him instantly. He went directly to heaven where he met Saint Peter at the gate. "How did you get here?" was the immediate question. "In two!" answered the golfer.

A group of people who always seem to overemphasize the importance of their score are those I refer to loosely as "cheaters." Those of you who are new to golf probably can't understand why anybody would cheat at a game. And yet golf, more than any sport I know, can bring out the "worst" in people. I know some people who can't count, others who are always improving their lie (especially in the rough), more than a fair share whose handicaps are not believable, and still others who interpret rules to fit their own needs.

Why do people who feel a need to cheat, rant and rave, or make themselves and others miserable play golf? I suspect because they think golf is only about how they score and they haven't ever asked themselves, "Why do I play golf?" This is a question you need to answer for yourself—whether you are a beginner or a low handicapper—if you hope to enjoy golf more and achieve the results you desire.

A few years ago, when Dr. Norman Vincent Peale and I wrote *The Power of Ethical Management,* we developed what we called the "Five P's [Principles] of Ethical Power."[1] I'm convinced that these principles are also the ingredients for personal power and genuine, lasting fulfillment in life. Highly successful, satisfied individuals practice these Five Principles of Personal Power with great consistency. I have found them very helpful in thinking about why I play golf and where golf fits into my life.

*

The
Five P's
Of
Personal
Power:

Purpose
Pride
Patience
Persistence
Perspective

*

The First Principle—Purpose

The five principles start with *purpose*. This is your intention—something toward which you are always striving. *A goal is not a purpose*. Goals are tangible and achievable. For example, you can have goals to improve your handicap, win your flight at your country club, get into a certain flight in your member/guest tournament, or feel good enough about your golf game to play with your spouse at a well-known resort course.

A goal has a beginning and an end. A purpose is ongoing. For example, I have four ongoing purposes for playing golf. First of all, to have fun; second, to enjoy people; third, to appreciate the beauty around me; and fourth, to compete against myself and others.

To have fun, I have to hit enough good shots and play enough good holes to be able to take pleasure in recalling them after the round at the "nineteenth hole." I recently got an eagle 3 on the par 5 seventeenth hole at the Pauma Valley Country Club, my home course in California. A 9-iron that I hit up the hill over a huge sand trap ended up in the cup. While I didn't play particularly well that day, the experience of first being unable to find my ball on the green and then seeing it wedged against the flag in the hole made my day—indeed my week! It was an exhilarating experience and gave me "bragging rights" after the round. That was fun!

To enjoy people, I need to play with folks who take the game seriously but themselves lightly. Laughing and kidding on the course are a must for me. That is why I seldom play alone and avoid people who cheat, act like spoiled brats, or in any way take themselves too seriously. I love the saying:

*

*You
Never
Own Golf;
It's
Only
On
Loan,
So
Enjoy It
While
You
Can*

*

If you believe that's true, as I do, then you can never take golf too seriously. Just when you lose it—you're playing poorly; you find it—you par the last three holes. Just when you find it—you're playing better than you ever have before; you lose it—you hit one out-of-bounds. You have to laugh or they'll come and take you away in a straitjacket. I want to play with people who realize the absurdity of this part of the game and laugh when others would cry or throw clubs.

To appreciate the beauty around me, I enjoy playing beautiful golf courses, particularly if I don't have to ride in a golf cart and can walk. That's why I love to play in Scotland or Ireland, where it's almost impossible to find a golf cart. As Shivas Irons, the magical Scottish golf professional whom Michael Murphy meets in *Golf in the Kingdom,* said, "The gemme is meant for walkin'."[2] And yet, even when we do get a chance to walk, most of us become so preoccupied with the next shot that we miss "the walkin' part." As Irons appropriately warns:

> *'Tis a shame, 'tis a rotten shame, for if ye can enjoy the walkin', ye can probably enjoy the other times in yer life when ye're in between, and that's most o' the time; wouldn't ye say?*[3]

I've thought a lot about all the modern technology that was supposed to make our lives simpler—fax machines, voice mail, car phones, etc. . . . . To me, these so-called "advances" have made my life more complicated. There are so many ways people can get to me today and ruin all my "in-between" times—driving in a car, eating a meal, and the like. That makes me love golf even more. I look at all my time on the course as in-between time. When I do drive in a golf cart, I make a concerted effort to take time, on the tee and when I walk off the green, to stop, look around, and take in the beauty. Otherwise, I can get caught up in a pattern of hitting my shot, then jumping in the cart and running to the next shot. In the process I miss this important purpose for playing golf.

I had a golfing high last year when I played the front nine at Pebble Beach with my wife, Margie. She had gained enough confidence in her game that she was willing, for the first time, to play on a major course. Coming off the sixth green together and seeing that panoramic view of the ocean was a peak experience. And then when Margie got a birdie on the par 3 fourth hole the next day at Spanish Bay, a Scottish-like links course, I knew she was hooked forever.

My son Scott's first real golfing thrill came when we got to play together with Charles Morris, a business colleague and friend from Savannah, at the Augusta National Golf Club, the home of the Masters Championship. Gary Player captured the essence of Augusta when he said:

> *When I think of Augusta I think of great beauty. I don't know of a golf course where you have such tremendous beauty anywhere in the world. And I've always said that if they have a course like this in heaven I hope I'm the head pro there one day.*[4]

It didn't really matter what Scott and I shot. Just being at Augusta and soaking in the beauty was enough.

A marvelous senior pro by the name of Dean Lind is on our teaching staff of the Golf University. Dean's love for the great game of golf goes back a long way. He beat Ken Venturi in the finals of the first United States Junior Amateur Championship in 1947. Since then he has played as a professional in tournaments all over the world. Dean feels that we often understate the sheer beauty of the game itself and the grandeur of its surroundings.

I'd like to quote from a note he sent to me:

> *I've always looked at the form of the game as one where the player could blend with nature . . . where one could create beautiful shots that matched the beauty of the surroundings. I can recall playing places like Geneva, Switzerland Country Club where the French Alps framed every shot; or Casa de Campo in the Dominican Republic where 6 holes rival the scenic nobility of #16 at Cypress Point; or Rose Garden Golf Club in Bangkok, Thailand, where the preponderance of floral displays rivals anything I've seen this side of the Queen's garden.*

I think Dean is right on. To me, the beauty of the surroundings becomes particularly captivating when it serves as background for the flight of a well-struck shot. Arnold Palmer expressed it well:

*

What Other People Find in
Poetry or Art Museums,
I Find in The Flight
Of A Good Drive:
The White Ball Sailing
Up Into The Blue Sky,
Reaching Its Apex,
Falling and
Finally
Dropping to the Turf . . .
Just the Way
I Planned It.

To compete against myself and others, I need to be constantly striving to improve. When I compete against myself, I like "medal play." Medal play is where you keep track of every shot on every hole and then add up your total at the end of the round to get your score. Most professional and amateur tournaments are won or lost on medal score. The pro with the lowest total score over three or four rounds wins. When I play medal I am concentrating on my total score. As I'll explain in Part Three, I set my own par (say, 84) and try to make that score. Medal play in golf is one of the most challenging games ever, because every swing counts, and therefore one bad hole can come back to haunt you when you add up your score at the end. Ben Hogan explained this well one day when someone tried to convince him that baseball was a tougher game than golf. His disagreement with this opinion was straightforward and to the point: "In golf you have to play your foul balls."

It's a real challenge to keep yourself together mentally over an eighteen-hole round that takes four or five hours to play and not lose your concentration on one or two holes and blow your score. It takes great self-discipline to get into trouble (as will happen) and not let what might be a bogey turn into an 8 or 9 score for the hole.

I also enjoy competing against other people who like to "do battle." Now I shift my attention from my score to focusing on how well I can play against someone else, or together with a partner against another team. When competing against others I like "match play." This is where you play a separate match against your opponent on every hole. The winner at the end of a round is determined by which player or team wins the most holes. The Ryder Cup, in which U.S. professionals play against their counterparts from Europe, is a match play tournament. It is an exciting event because a high score on one hole doesn't put you out of a match. There is always the next hole.

When I compete against others, I like to have something at stake. If it's a championship or a pro-am event, how I do or how my team does compared to the rest of the field is enough. If there is no tournament, I like to make a small wager.

During the summer I have a favorite group I like to play with at the Skaneateles Country Club near our cottage in upstate New York. The reason I enjoy playing with these people is because they all love to compete and play well, but they don't take themselves seriously. We make all kinds of fun bets. The money is not important because the winners always throw their "earnings" into the center of the table at the end of the match to pay for the lunch. Our bets are meant only to motivate everyone to play their best and always stay in the game.

We usually play $2 Nassau (a $2 match for the front nine, a $2 match for the back nine, and a $2 match for the eighteen holes) with a "press" available (a new $2 match) when any team is two holes down on the front nine or back nine match. So, if you are two holes down going into the ninth hole, you can press your opponents and start a new match that is worth the same as the entire nine-hole match. A win on the last hole can even the match. We also play some fun side bets we call "garbage." For example, we pay $2 for a "sandie" (getting a par from a sand trap), a "barkie" (getting a par after hitting a tree—but there must still be bark on your ball when you take it out of the cup), or a "greenie" (getting closest to the pin on par 3's). In addition, we pay $2 for a "birdie" (one under par). On a rare occasion someone has had a "barkie, sandie, birdie," which pays the *big* sum of $6.

When I was a kid my dad and I played nine holes almost every night in the summer when he got home from work. My mom would have sandwiches ready, and off we would go with the golf-playing neighbors. My dad loved to play "bingle, bangle, bongle"—you could win a point (worth 10 cents) for *first on* the green (bingle), *closest* to the pin (bangle), and *first in* the cup (bongle).

"Bingle, bangle, bongle" is a great equalizer because you can win "first on" with a 6 or 7 or more and, no matter what your handicap, you can win "closest" to the hole or "first in." The kidding in this game is nonstop too. No matter what you do, your opponents claim you just are setting yourself up for a "bingle," "bangle," or "bongle." My dad, who seldom broke 100, could beat anyone at "bingle, bangle, bongle." It was an enjoyable way to compete, with very little money actually changing hands. In fact, when I was young my dad told me the story of a wealthy man who suggested a $2 Nassau to a foursome at his club. A young, aggressive new member said, "Let's make it worth our time and play a $10 Nassau."

The wealthy man said, "If the stakes are not high enough, let's play a $500 Nassau."

The young golfer was taken aback. He said, "I can't afford a $500 Nassau."

"Well, I can," said the wealthy man. "So let's play for $2."

In summary, golf is a unique experience that is difficult to characterize to the satisfaction of all. There are certainly many more reasons to play golf than the ones I have chosen. What is (are) your purpose(s)? Why do you play golf? These are questions you need to answer and then observe and monitor your behavior to see how well you are doing in relation to your purpose(s). Sometimes people say they play golf for one reason and then their behavior does not follow. You will enjoy the game most if your behavior is aligned with your purpose(s) for playing.

The Second Principle—Pride

Why do people get "off purpose" and cheat and throw clubs on the golf course? The answer may be in the second principle—*pride*. It is healthy and justified to feel good about yourself and your accomplishments. That's what pride is all about. Some people, however, have too much or too little pride. A sense of superiority or inferiority often plays itself out in one of two ways, either of which can have an impact on your behavior on the course: false pride or self-doubt.

False pride is a negative kind of pride that occurs when people have a distorted image of their own importance. Nothing can get us off course quicker than false pride—it blurs our purpose. We start to think we should always win or always be on top of everything. People with false pride regard themselves as the center of all things. In golf, their constant desire to win can motivate them to cheat, exaggerate, argue, or rationalize. They will do anything to avoid looking bad. Their pride can't allow them to lose and their egos suffer when they do.

I once played with a top manager who organized a company golf outing around his ego. He organized the bets, he got the best partner, and he became upset if the tee markers were back too far or the pin placements were too difficult. If he expressed his displeasure, people would be running around trying to fix things. Everybody was uncomfortable and tried to avoid playing with him.

People with self-doubt, on the other hand, don't trust their own judgment and appear to have low self-esteem. On a golf course they always downplay their ability and put themselves down. They appear to be defeated before they start. They take golf almost too seriously and use their bad performance as one more indication of their "not OKness": "I can't play golf." They also are not very much fun to be around.

It is easy to understand that self-doubt comes from lack of self-esteem, but it is harder to believe that false pride is also a result of low self-esteem. People who act like they always have to be Number One, and who always need to be on center stage, are often thought of as having inflated egos. The reality is that people with false pride, who act as if only *they* count and others not at all, are really trying to make up for their own "I don't count" feelings. If people don't feel good about themselves, they often overcompensate for those "not OK" feelings by trying to control everything and everybody. For them, golf is just one more thing that has to be controlled.

If you are truthful with yourself and suspect that you have false pride or self-doubt and it manifests itself in your golf game—what can you do about it? You can focus on the *positive* instead of the negative.

Every time you play golf you have two choices. You can feel good about yourself and the game or you can feel lousy. Why choose the latter? To me:

*

The
Worst
A
Game
Of
Golf
Can Be
Is
Great!

*

You can always find something you feel good about. Catch yourself doing something right and you will be amazed how you will start to do more things that are right. Once you get down on yourself in golf, you are through. When was the last time you caught yourself doing something right on the golf course? Most people never praise themselves. Even when an opponent says to them, "Nice shot," they discount the compliment by saying, "I wish I could say I was aiming there," or "I didn't get it all." One Minute Praisings are not just for other people; they're also for you to use on yourself.

When you make a mistake, I like the phrase "*How unlike me* . . . to have missed that putt, or . . . to have lost my concentration on that last hole, or . . . whatever"! If you're not your own best friend, who is? While feeling good about yourself is important, don't get carried away. That might also lead to false pride. Remember, the universe does not center around you; you are part of a bigger universe. Put your golf game in that kind of perspective.

Larry Moody, director of Search Ministries, who runs the Wednesday night Bible study on the PGA tour, teaches the golfers who worship with him the importance of keeping their egos under control. The work Moody has done with these players is described in an article entitled "The Modern Crusade" in the March 1988 *Golf Digest* magazine. In talking about self-esteem, Moody often quotes Philippians 2:3:

> *Do nothing out of selfish ambition or vain conceit, but in humility consider others better than yourselves.*

Moody's congregation includes Paul Azinger, Bernard Langer, Larry Mize, Larry Nelson, Corey Pavin, Scott Simpson—all of whom get their egos out of the way. That is particularly important for them, since ego could be said to stand for "*Edging God Out.*"

The Third Principle—Patience

Once you have a clear purpose for playing golf and your ego is under control, the third principle necessary to enjoy and play better golf is *patience*. One way you can get "off purpose" with your golf game is to lose faith and become impatient when things go wrong early in a round. That impatience not only affects your "on purpose" behavior, but it also keeps you from reaching your goals.

As I have listened to top teachers and golfers over the years, the one quality they suggest we can all use more of is patience. Norman Vincent Peale feels that positive thinking is an important aspect of patience. When things aren't going right, patience is an energized belief that things will eventually go your way. As a result, you don't give up and start to cheat or lose control or begin to take uncalled-for risks to get the *results* you want right *now*. Let me give you a personal example to show you how patience and positive thinking can help in golf.

I was playing a round one day at Pala Mesa, the beautiful resort course in San Diego County where we first housed our Golf University. It's a challenging course for someone like me who hits the ball from right to left and is constantly fighting a hook. I feel good if I break 85 on this course.

This particular day I made par on the first hole—an uphill par 5. The second hole is a short par 4, but it is a tough driving hole because it not only has a severe out-of-bounds to the left down an embankment, but also does not have a lot of room on the right before you're in deep rough. This day, I hit the perfect drive. I just marveled while watching it sail right to the center of the fairway. I don't know what it hit—a rock or a broken sprinkler head, but when it landed, the ball suddenly ricocheted to the left out-of-bounds. A perfect drive and I'm out-of-bounds.

I could have thrown a club or stomped around and let that ruin my whole round. But I had been working on patience. So I stepped back, took a deep breath, and hit another drive, which landed on the fairway. I got a double bogey 6 on a hole I should have parred, but I knew I had sixteen holes left to play.

If you are patient it's amazing how things work out. When we came to the eighth hole, I hit another good drive on a dogleg right par 4. I hit a 7-iron for my second shot, but pulled it dead left. The ball headed straight toward a big tree alongside the green. I would be lucky if it didn't end up out-of-bounds or "in jail" (I would have no shot for the green) behind the tree. Instead the ball hit in the middle of the tree and ricocheted out toward the center of the green and landed two feet from the cup for an easy birdie. I shot 82 that day and felt great. But if I hadn't been patient with my game, I could have lost my temper on the second hole, forgotten why I play golf, and carried on about the bad luck I was having. In the process I would have sabotaged my score that day as well as taken what was supposed to be an enjoyable afternoon and turned it into a nightmare.

With people who play golf for a living, patience is all-important. In fact, I've seen patience time and again be the winning factor in major tournaments. Curtis Strange's winning of his second U.S. Open in a row at the Oakhill Country Club in Rochester, New York, in 1989 is a good example of patience. In the final round he didn't have a birdie for sixteen holes. In the meantime, everyone else was having trouble. When he really needed a birdie, it came on the seventeenth hole. He said patience won it for him.

I also remember Sandy Lyle's winning of the Masters in 1988. It looked like he had the tournament wrapped up on the tenth hole, but suddenly he bogeyed 11 and double bogeyed 12 (two of the holes called "Amen Corner"). Suddenly the announcers and everybody seemed to count him out even though he only went from 2 up on the field to 1 down. Lyle was patient with himself and hung in there, and he was able to fight his way back to a tie with Mark Calcavecchia going into the eighteenth hole. Lyle then hit his tee shot too far, ending up with a tough bunker lie about 160 yards from the pin. Again Lyle was patient and didn't lose his cool. He hit one of the greatest shots in golf history to within ten feet of the pin and then knocked the putt in for the win. He could have given up on the twelfth hole but his patience paid off. He never got down on himself.

When you are patient, you have a different way of looking at things. You don't always have to have what you want right away. Impatience—having to have things happen now—often results in poor decision making. You start to cheat, break the rules, behave poorly, or try to make up for a bad break by taking an unwarranted chance. That leads me to the next principle—*persistence.*

The Fourth Principle—Persistence

Without *persistence,* patience is not sufficient to keep you on track. You can't just wait for good to come your way. You have to take action. It's like the man who, every night for six months, had prayed to the Lord to let him win the lottery—but nothing happened. He became impatient. The next night when he knelt to pray, he was angry. He said to the Lord, "I can't understand why I haven't won the lottery yet. I've prayed every night for six months for it. I am a good person. I love my wife, I am good to my kids, and faithful to You. Why haven't I won the lottery yet?"

There was a crack of lightning in the sky and a voice shouted down: "Give me a hand. Buy a ticket!"

In golf, taking action means having a plan and sticking to it. For example, suppose you normally expect to score 5 on the toughest par 4 on the course. In fact, you would be pleased with a bogey. Yet, it is tempting, when you are 200 yards away, to try to hit a career shot over a creek to a well-protected green, and suffer the consequences of an impatient, risky decision. The prudent approach would be to stroke a 9-iron and set up your third shot for your bogey. This is all about stick-to-itiveness!

Persistence also applies to your purpose. If your purpose includes having fun, enjoying the comradeship and the beauty of the course, then observing your behavior as you compete with yourself and others will help you decide if what you are doing is "on purpose." If it isn't, make adjustments.

The Fifth Principle—Perspective

The last principle is *perspective*—the capacity to see what is really important in any given situation. The LPGA tour this last year produced a heartwarming perspective story. The year before, Shelly Hamblin was diagnosed with cancer and there was fear she might not pull through. Not only did Shelly pull through, she won one of the first tournaments she entered upon her return to the tour.

When asked about this triumph, not only over her fellow competitors but her illness, Shelly was very reflective. She related how she was enjoying every day more than ever before. And golf had taken on a new perspective for her, too. Before she got sick, Shelly thought a three-foot putt was life or death; now that she knows more about death, three-foot putts look very different. They seem easier to make. Shelly's renewed vigor for life and perspective on golf are inspirational.

Rabbi Harold Kushner, author of the best-selling *When Bad Things Happen to Good People*, took perspective one step further for me in his follow-up book, *When All You've Ever Wanted Isn't Enough*. He said that in all his years as a rabbi he never heard anyone on their deathbed say, "I wish I had gone to the office more." I doubt if any of them said, "I wish I had played better golf" either. They all wished they had loved more and spent more time with the people they cared about. In golf, like life, we can fool ourselves into thinking it's all about results, that who we are is what we accomplish. Instead we should remember that golf stands for:

*

*Game
Of
Life
First*

*

How true that statement becomes when you realize that golf, like life, is a game where you can get some good breaks and bad breaks you don't deserve—and good breaks and bad breaks you do deserve. Sometimes you are playing better than you expect and you have to deal with success. At other times, you are playing worse than you expect and you have to deal with failure. And all this occurs within a period of four or five hours—one round of golf—with the focus all on YOU. The little ball sits there and waits for you to move it.

Friend, fellow author *(Golfer's Stroke-Saving Handbook)*, and golf nut Roy Benjamin says it well:

> *You are a fortunate person, indeed, if you can begin each day accepting the fact that during that day there will be ups and downs, good breaks and bad ones, disappointments, surprises, unexpected turns of events. At the same time wise golfers have learned to accept those adverse conditions on the golf course as representative of real life challenges.*[5]

So what better training ground is there for learning to accept the bitter with the sweet than the golf course, where on one occasion your drive may hit the cart path and fly fifty yards down the fairway and on another ricochet out-of-bounds.

Michael Murphy, in his classic book *Golf in the Kingdom*, catches this sentiment perfectly:

> *How often have we seen a round go from an episode out of The Three Stooges to the agonies of King Lear—perhaps in the space of one hole! I will never forget a friend who declared after his tee shot that he wanted to kill himself but when the hole was finished, said with total sincerity, that he had never been so happy in his entire life. No other game is more capable of evoking a person's total commitment.*[6]

While all this may sound like golf is 50/50 between bitter and sweet, it's not even close to that distribution. I'd rather use Yogi Berra-type math: Golf is 50 percent bitter and the other 90 percent is sweet. As Roy Benjamin insists:

> *If, as the poet said, "Life is a game," then it is a game played much better and more rewardingly because several centuries ago a group of simple Scotsmen, with perhaps unwitting wisdom, saw the joy to be derived and the lessons to be learned by combining a stick and a pellet, the challenges of terrain and nature, and a hole in the ground.*[7]

You can learn a lot about yourself from golf. I guarantee if you cheat or blow up when you get a bad break or make a mistake, that behavior will show up in other parts of your life. If you maintain a positive attitude in golf, even when things are going sour, I bet that will carry over to other things too.

When I play beautiful courses where my awareness is heightened and the flight of the ball becomes something to marvel at, I achieve serenity and can step back and smell the roses.

For me, that serenity can be reached when I am able to get outside myself and take what friend and colleague Morris Massey calls a "mental helicopter" to the ceiling to a viewing point. There you can look down at yourself and watch the happenings as a participant-observer in your own life.

I find that I am able to have that experience more when playing golf than while engaged in any other activity. During those times I am able to keep my ego under control and gain perspective. Then why I play golf becomes increasingly clear. So perspective brings us back to purpose. Why do *you* play the great game of golf?

*

*I Have Loved Playing the
Game and Practicing It.
Whether My Schedule for
The Following Day Called
For a Tournament Round or
Merely a Trip to the Practice Tee,
The Prospect That There was
Going to be Golf in It
Made Me Feel Privileged
and Extremely Happy.
I couldn't Wait for the
Sun to Come Up so
That I Could Get Out
On the Course Again.*
—**Ben Hogan**

*

CHAPTER 2
Goal Setting: What Do You Want to Accomplish?

Golf is like a love affair.
If you don't take it seriously,
It's not any fun.
If you take it seriously,
It will break your heart.
—Arthur Daly
Sports columnist

While a purpose is ongoing—something toward which you are always striving—a goal is tangible and achievable. It has a beginning and an end.

There are two types of goals in golf: results, or *performance goals*, and fun, or *satisfaction goals*. Performance goals tend to be more objective and outcome oriented. Success depends on results—how well you did compared to par, your handicap, or your opponent(s). While the emphasis in golf has been on performance goals, they are not relevant to all golfers or to any one golfer all of the time. Some people play for satisfaction goals. These goals tend to be more subjective and fun oriented. That's not to say you can't have fun shooting a good round—you sure can! The distinction I'm trying to make is that success in satisfaction goals does not depend on results, but on emotions and feelings: how well you enjoyed the people in your foursome, the course, and the setting; if you were able to stay calm and let bad shots go and enjoy good ones.

I usually have both performance goals and satisfaction goals. If, however, I am in a highly competitive situation, I will lean toward performance goals. On other occasions, when I am playing with family or good friends, I might focus on satisfaction goals. Which direction you go and the kinds of goals you set will determine how seriously you are going to take the game and, therefore, how vulnerable you are to the broken heart that Arthur Daly mentions. But remember:

*

*You
Are
the Sole Judge
of
Your
Goals*

*Don't
Dance
to
Someone Else's
Music*

*

Since all good performance starts with clear goals, the first secret of being a performance- and/or satisfaction-oriented golfer is One Minute Goal Setting.

Setting SMART Goals

As you set goals around your golf game, make sure each of those goals is SMART. This is an acronym for the most important factors in setting quality goals: *S*pecific, *M*otivational, *A*ttainable, *R*elevant, and *T*rackable.[1]

SPECIFIC. Just saying you want to improve or enjoy golf more over the next six months is not a clear goal. It is not specific enough. What do you mean by "improve"—is it a lower score or handicap, or beating a certain opponent? What do you mean by "enjoying golf more"—is it being comfortable playing with your spouse or playing on a certain course? The more specific you can be about a goal and the more you can observe and count it, the better. To improve your game or enjoy golf more, you must know what an achieved goal will look like—and what constitutes progress toward that goal.

Whether you set a *practice goal,* a *long-range goal* (six months), a *short-range goal* (this round), or an *immediate goal* (the next shot), each of your goals should be observable and measurable if you are to make progress. Let me give you some examples:

PRACTICE GOALS

—When you come off the practice tee, how do you know if you had a good session? How many 9-irons did you hit? What percentage went toward the target you were aiming at? Did you have fun? How do you know? Was it a beautiful setting? Did you have a few laughs with others who were practicing too? On a 1-to-10 scale, how did you feel? Were you happy to be alive?

LONG-RANGE GOALS

—Suppose your handicap is 25, which means you shoot around 100. What is your goal in six months? Do you eventually want to play in the 80's or will you be happy to reach 100 on a regular basis? If you presently shoot in the 80's, would you like to shoot in the 70's? Suppose you're a beginner. What is realistic for you to be shooting in six months? If you want to enjoy golf more, what will make that happen? Would you be playing with your spouse once a week? Would you have gone to play in Scotland or felt comfortable enough to play in the Thursday night league at your course? Would you have learned not to let bad shots devastate you?

SHORT-RANGE GOALS

—You're having a drink after a round. Are you pleased with your score or the way you played? Did you have fun? How do you know? Were you playing with your favorite foursome on one of your favorite courses? How were you feeling?

IMMEDIATE GOALS

—You have a 6-iron in your hand and you are 150 yards from the hole. What would a good shot look like? Is your goal only results (where the ball lands) or does it include trajectory (height and direction of flight)? How could you have fun hitting this shot?

My father had a friend, Eddie Levine, who played with us all the time when I was a kid. He was a perfect example of someone who didn't worry about traditional golfing goals. If he hit his drive to the right off the tee he might head off to the left in search of his ball. My father would say, "Eddie! You hit it to the right." Eddie would respond, with a twinkle in his eye, "Does it really matter?" He never spent much time looking for a lost ball.

You might think Eddie didn't have any clear, measurable goals. Well, he did! They were mainly fun-and-satisfaction goals that had little to do with how he scored. If you had asked Eddie to describe a good round of golf, he would have been quick to say:

- Getting at least two pars per nine holes
- Enjoying a cigar or two on the course
- Playing with friends who don't take themselves or the game too seriously
- Having a relaxed lunch and a few beers after the round

Eddie didn't care so much where he played; he was more concerned with whom he played and the enjoyment he experienced. His goals were unique to him and he was very purposeful about achieving them. You should do the same for yourself:

*

*Measure
What
You Want
From
Your Golf Game.*

*

MOTIVATIONAL. That statement and Eddie Levine's philosophy lead perfectly into the second aspect of goal setting. For you to accomplish a goal, it has to be a goal that *motivates you*. A friend of ours wanted his wife to be an avid golfer. He pushed her to play in the eighteen-hole ladies' group, even though she had always been content to be in a more casual nine-hole group. Each day she played, he asked her about her score, what she had learned, the number of putts she had taken, etc. She could never answer these questions. She was more interested in the social experience. As a result, she never became an avid golfer. Obviously what was motivating to him about golf—i.e. improving his score—was not motivating to her.

Making sure that your goals are motivational gives you tremendous latitude whether you are practicing or playing. For example, one of my friends spent most of his practice time on the driving range trying to hit "the big one" with his driver. And yet, the part of his game that needed the most work was his short game. He lost all kinds of strokes around the green, but that didn't matter to him. It just wasn't any fun to practice pitching, chipping, putting, and sand play. And besides, he evaluated his round by how many times he outdrove his friends rather than outscored them. That all changed when he started playing with an old college buddy who moved into town. When they had been in school together, they were fierce competitors in everything they did. It didn't take many humiliating losses to motivate my friend to come to the Short Game School at the Golf University and begin to practice around the greens.

So it is important to remember that the thing that motivates you might fluctuate from situation to situation. For example, sometimes when you are playing you might be motivated by shooting for a particular score, while at other times you couldn't care less about your score. When I play with my wife, Margie, and it's a particularly long course, she'll keep score on some holes and not on others. If she finds herself getting behind or battling the rough, she may pick up her ball and carry it to where I'm hitting my next shot. Sometimes I'll give myself the liberty of hitting a second shot when the first one goes astray. When we play together, we don't want to make golf a hassle. Other times, when we play with another couple who take the game a little more seriously, or when either of us play in a league or some competitive event, we keep an accurate score.

Recently we devised a special program in Team Building and Golf for a client. Michael O'Connor, a top behavioral scientist, and I wanted to create for this company a team-building experience as stimulating and motivating as outdoor activities like rock climbing and river rafting have been for other companies. As the final part of a three-year management development program that Michael had run for the Holt Companies of Texas, we divided the managers into 6 four-member teams. Each team had one "A," "B," "C," and "D" golfer, the ranking done according to each golfer's ability and experience with the game. In most cases, the "A" player shot in the 80's, while the "D" player had never played golf before. As a result, every team had golfers with a variety of skills and competencies.

Having learned the key concepts from *The One Minute Manager Builds High Performing Teams,* each team was then given the task of building its own high performing team. The laboratory to make that happen was the golf course.

Nine-hole team activities were planned over a three-day period; every team was required to use a shot from each member on every hole where the team's score was 4 or above. Staff members from the Golf University were available in between events to work with various teams on their skill development. It was fun to watch the teams plan, organize, motivate, and control how they functioned.

With the pressure to utilize every member, the teams learned quickly how to encourage and support each other. For example, Peter Holt, president of the Holt Companies, was a new golfer. It was a real delight to watch his team help him line up and negotiate a crucial four-foot putt, and then to hear Peter shout with joy when he made the putt as his team members raced over to congratulate him. Peter Holt said, "That was an exciting moment for everyone on our team."

Ann Cass, a new golfer, related: "I loved the support that I got from my team. They had no choice; they had to utilize my talents so the support I got from everyone was wonderful. In fact, this experience is motivating me to become a golfer." That seemed to be a common reaction. Moreover, when the golfing activities were over, people wished they could do them again.

Motivation is the key to learning and enjoying golf. And it will also have an impact on the kind of goals you set. Sid Cohen, chairman of the board of Norstan, a telecommunications company in Minneapolis, is a senior golfer in his 70's. When he and his senior friends come to a 200-yard par 3 hole, they just take their balls to about 150 yards from the hole and play their tee shots from there. "Who are we trying to kid?" says Sid. "Golf is supposed to be fun, not work. As you get older you just have to change your expectations and modify the game accordingly."

ATTAINABLE. Sid's comments are well taken. For a goal to be motivating, you need to feel you can accomplish it. If a goal is constantly out of reach, the game will soon get discouraging. Professor David McClelland[2] and others did some interesting research at Harvard University a number of years ago on achievement motivation. For example, they found that high achievers set goals differently than other people. They took a group of people and handed them, one by one, several rings and asked them to go into a room and toss the rings at a stake. It was like the old ring-toss game, with one important difference. The people could toss the rings any distance they wanted from the stake. There was no line that they could not cross. The study noted the differences in behavior.

Two groups of people didn't want to be evaluated. The first group, when given the rings, would go very close to the stake—almost on top of it—and toss the rings. What was wrong with their goals? They were too easy.

The second group of people who didn't want to be evaluated took the rings far from the stake and started tossing them over their shoulders or behind their backs at the stake. What was wrong with their goals? They were too difficult.

When people already identified as high achievers entered the room, however, they would inch slowly toward the stake. Then they would stop and throw a few rings. If they made most of the tosses, they would move back. If they missed most of the tosses, they would move forward. High achievers wanted to find out at what distance from the stake could they make most of the tosses but not all of them. They liked to push themselves. They liked to set stretching goals that are moderately difficult yet achievable.

So setting a goal of just breaking 90 in a round does not make sense if you're continually shooting in the low 80's—the goal is too easy. It is also inappropriate to play against par 72 if you are a 15 handicapper—the goal is too difficult. If you are shooting mostly in the low 90's, a round of 89 would be a stretching, but attainable, goal.

Whatever goal you set, whether it be a performance or a satisfaction goal, you have to ask, "How badly do I want to achieve this goal?" "What is my commitment?" These questions will affect whether your goal is attainable.

RELEVANT. This aspect of goal setting is particularly important for learning or practicing golf. Most golfers—whether beginners or experienced players—want to learn everything all at once as soon as they decide to improve their score. Unfortunately, teaching professionals, golf schools, golf magazines, and golf videos are quite accommodating to that desire. Too many times they overload you with an excess of information and techniques to incorporate into your golf game all at once. When this occurs, "paralysis by analysis" sets in. You can't swing because you have too many things you are working on!

Good learning goals are relevant—focused on the areas that can make the most difference. All of Dr. Charles Garfield's research[3] on high performance shows that peak performers focus on only a few goals—three to five maximum. Remember the 80/20 rule: 80 percent of the results you desire come from 20 percent of all the behavior involved. In golf, you want to limit the number of goals during one period of time. If you are working on the mechanical part of your game, concentrate on no more than three goals on the full swing—balance, weight shift, follow-through—and no more than three goals on the short game—alignment, tempo, body movement.

For beginners, perhaps a single goal related to each of the different aspects of the game might be appropriate: driving, chipping, putting, and so on. For example, if you are a beginner, and practicing your full swing, you might focus just on shifting your weight to the right side on your backswing and shifting it to the left side on your forward swing (left-handers would do the opposite). When you are working on weight shift, you might not want to worry about any other aspect of your swing.

Relevance is a major issue when it comes to your short game. It is estimated that about 67 percent of all shots in golf are taken from closer than forty yards from the hole. Are you spending 67 percent of your practice time on your short game? How about putting? If you analyze it, a par 72 has one half of the strokes assigned to putting (par 5's equal 2 putts, par 4's equal 2 putts, and par 3's equal 2 putts). There is no reason why any amateur player can't average 36 putts a round or less. Good putting does not require strength or athletic ability. Yet if you miss short putts—even one short putt—it can be devastating to your score and to your psychology. How often do you practice putting?

In setting satisfaction goals, relevance is a key too. What are the most important ingredients that determine whether you enjoy golf? Concentrate on making sure those ingredients are part of the game. Remember, you are the judge of relevance. Chuck Hogan states it well:

*Do You
Play
to
Enjoy Golf
or
Do You
Enjoy Yourself
While
You Play Golf?*

TRACKABLE. Once you have a way to measure goal accomplishment, take time to monitor and record your progress. In other words, find a way to keep score on how well you are doing. If you don't take time to measure and compare your progress, your goals and corresponding behavior will soon become unfocused and no clear progress will be evident. For example:

> As you practice getting out of a sand trap, every ten shots record the number of times you make a complete follow-through on your swing. Don't stop until you make ten swings in a row, each with a full follow-through.

> After each hole, rate yourself on a 1-to-10 scale on how well you managed your emotions. Did you get angry or upset? How did that affect the way you played? Track your evaluations for the next six rounds.

> How many times in the last month did you accomplish your performance goals? How about your satisfaction goals? Is your percentage improving or getting worse?

Remember, performance goals tend to be more objective, while satisfaction goals are more subjective. That makes it harder to measure and monitor satisfaction goals. But if you want to enjoy golf more, you have to find a way to determine how well you are doing.

If you know what you want to accomplish in terms of performance or satisfaction goals, you can stay on track by monitoring your behavior and patting yourself on the back when you make progress. Except for an immediate goal (this shot), all your goals in golf have to be reached over time—six months, this eighteen-hole round, this practice session. Tracking progress keeps you focused and realistic. John Darling, one of our pioneer teachers at the Golf University, makes our students think twice when he says, "To improve from a 25 handicapper to a 10 you first have to go from 25 to 24, and then from 24 to 23, on down to 10." Tracking your progress tells you where you've been and where you still have to go.

Monitoring Your Practice

When you head to the practice area, it is important to decide if you are going to concentrate on behaviors or outcomes. What you have to do to hit a shot focuses on behaviors: grip, stance, position of head, weight shift, follow-through, etc. . . . Outcomes are the results of hitting the ball: distance, direction, height, accuracy, and so on.

If you're trying to learn to do something new, it's best to forget about the outcome and concentrate on behavior. At the Golf University when we work with beginners, we often don't let them hit any full swing shots the first morning so they don't get distracted by the outcome. We just have them take practice swings. Then with video feedback, we can zero in on the desired behavior in the student's swing. These desired behaviors, once learned, can encourage beginners rather than discourage them when they get to the practice tee. If you are practicing something new and you focus only on results, on where the ball goes, you can become discouraged.

Once you think you can perform the necessary behaviors or skills to execute a certain shot, you can then focus on outcomes or results. Start hitting balls and watch what happens. If you're getting the results you want, pat yourself on the back and keep doing what you've been doing. If, however, you don't like the results you are getting (you are hooking or slicing or hitting a shot too high or too low, for example), step back and try to discover what might be causing the undesirable results. You can then go back to redirection and focusing on behavior.

D. Swing Meyer, author of *The Method: A Golf Success Strategy*, has an innovative approach to learning golf that I think is an effective way to monitor your practice. He thinks that starting to learn the game by standing on the practice range and hitting 5-irons all over the place is programmed for failure. All you will get is sore hands and a shattered ego. Swing starts beginners with a ten-inch putt. That's what he did with his son:

> *My eleven-year-old son can set up and sink ten-inch putts all day long. If you asked him how good he was ten inches from the hole, he would say: "Great!" The very first time that kid ever played golf, he had only one experience—success. My first lesson with the youngster took twenty minutes. He spent that time ringing the success register. When he walked off the green, he turned to me and said, "Golf's a pretty easy game, isn't it, Dad?" It is easier if you start off on the right foot. . . .*[4]

I'll never forget an interview with a great bowler I saw on television once. He told the reporter he had started bowling when he was five years old.

"Didn't you get discouraged at first?" the reporter wondered. "At that age you would roll a lot of gutter balls."

"My father put a pin at the end of each gutter," smiled the champion, "so I never got discouraged. I loved bowling right from the start because whenever I rolled the ball I would always knock something down."

Swing Meyer thinks golf should be taught and learned in "bite-sized" increments. You start with a simple ten-inch putt and don't move back until that shot is *mastered.* What's attractive about this approach, according to Swing, is "golfers achieve immediate success, keep the door to self-doubt closed as long as possible, and develop at their own pace through a series of non-threatening 'mini games.'" This strategy starts with putting mastery, then moves to chipping and pitching mastery, followed by approach shot mastery and driver mastery.

What follows are the twenty-three steps to Swing Meyer's Mastery Game, containing the shot and mastery criteria.[5]

Swing Meyer's Mastery Game

Putting Mastering

Step	Shot	Mastery Criterion
1	10-inch putt	8 putts consecutively holed
2	16-inch putt	8 putts consecutively holed
3	2-foot putt	8 putts consecutively holed
4	3-foot putt	8 putts consecutively holed
5	4-foot putt, some break	4 holed, 4 out of 4 within 8 inches
6	6-foot putt	8 consecutively within 8 inches
7	10-foot putt	8 consecutively within 12 inches
8	15-foot putt	8 consecutively within 15 inches
9	20-foot putt	8 consecutively within 18 inches
10	30-foot putt	8 consecutively within 24 inches

Chipping and Pitching Mastery

11	35-foot chip from 5 feet off green	6 out of 8 within 6 feet
12	35-foot chip from 15 feet off green	6 out of 8 within 6 feet
13	65-foot chip from 5 feet off green	6 out of 8 within 6 feet
14	25-yard pitch	6 out of 8 within 10 feet
15	35-yard pitch	6 out of 8 within 15 feet
16	50-yard pitch	6 out of 8 within 15 feet
17	75-yard pitch	6 out of 8 within 30 feet

Approach Shot Mastery

18	100-yard shots	8 out of 10 within 40 feet
19	125-yard shots	8 out of 10 within 45 feet
20	150-yard shots	8 out of 10 within 54 feet
21	175-yard shots	8 out of 10 within 90 feet

Driver Mastery: Step 23

	250 yards	7 out of 10 within 40 yards
	225 yards	7 out of 10 within 35 yards
	200 yards	7 out of 10 within 22 yards
	175 yards	7 out of 10 within 22 yards
	150 yards	7 out of 10 within 18 yards

Let me make some comments about these steps. First, about 70 percent of the steps involve shots from 75 yards or less. This fact, plus having over 50 percent of these steps devoted to putting, correspond with the reality that the true action in golf centers around the short game. That's why we offer a special Short Game School at the Golf University. There are a lot of amateurs who can keep up with the pros off the tee and with the middle and long irons, but where they get left in the dust is on the short game. "The drive is for show but the putt is for dough" is a truthful adage. What do you practice and get instruction on the most?

Second, the actual criterion chosen for each of the steps is not as important as the fact that there are criteria. You can fill in your own criterion, but without some way to measure progress you can't "graduate" to the next level.

Third, the steps are a wonderful guide to developing a practice plan. Most people have no plan when they practice. They start off hitting a few wedges, then a few 9-irons, and gradually move through the bag until they get to the driver. When they get tired or reach some time limit, they quit. Seldom do they have any clear targets at which they are aiming or a way to evaluate how well they are doing with any one club. The old saying that is often attributed to the late great football coach George Allen is so true:

*

*Practice
Doesn't
Make
Perfect*

*Perfect
Practice
Makes
Perfect*

*

Adapting some learning or practice strategy like Swing Meyer's "mini-games" will help you set SMART practice goals that are *specific* (you know what you are practicing and can observe and measure how well you are doing), *motivational* (you can create a practice routine that is fun for you), *attainable* (you set the criteria), *relevant* (you can determine what parts of your game need work), and *trackable* (you can monitor progress).

Let me emphasize the motivational aspect of practice. Playing "games" while you practice will make it more fun. As you progress in your proficiencies, you can create your own mastery games for trouble shots like sand play, uphill, downhill lies, or any part of the game you want. *You are in charge.* Down the road you can practice hitting low-trajectory and high-trajectory shots. Make your practicing fun and appropriate for your needs. Kids do that all the time. One of them will hit a big slice. A friend will see it and say, "I bet I can hit a bigger slice than that." Pretty soon they're trying to bend a shot around a tree. Then they start trying to hook the ball. That's how they learn to hit every conceivable shot—in a fun way. Adults are too serious.

Monitoring Your Behavior

In the last chapter I suggested that people who cheat, rant and rave, and make themselves and others miserable on the golf course have probably never asked themselves, "Why do I play golf?" If they did, these people might never behave like that because they would be clear about their purpose in playing.

When people are behaving inappropriately on the golf course, it's usually because they are frustrated about how they are playing. Their game is not living up to their expectations—they are being blocking from achieving their goals. How can you catch yourself before you do things on the golf course you might later regret? Norman Vincent Peale and I developed a three-question Ethics Check[6] for our book *The Power of Ethical Management* that might help you decide the right thing to do.

The first Ethics Check question is straightforward. *Is it legal?* Every year the United States Golf Association (USGA) prints copies of the rules of golf, including any changes that may have been made during the previous year. Copies are readily available at a very reasonable price. Tom Watson and Peter Aliss were even commissioned by the USGA and the Royal and Ancient Golf Club of St. Andrews to make a video tape entitled *The Official Rules of Golf.* Everyone who plays golf should know the rules.

My inclination was to take the rules pretty casually until one summer when I was playing in a member/guest tournament at the Skaneateles Country Club in upstate New York. One of our opponents was a real stickler for the rules. Several times my partner and I lost strokes because we simply did not know a clearly stated USGA rule. For example, it started to rain. While my partner was putting, I held an umbrella over his head. That seemed like a kind, considerate thing to do. However, there is a clear rule against giving such help. After that match, which we lost, I vowed I would study the USGA rules.

Is it always necessary to play by the USGA rules? No! You can invent your own rules as long as everyone you are playing with agrees with those rules and as long as what you are doing is not damaging the course or taking away from anyone else's enjoyment of the game. Kerry Graham, a top teacher and president of the LPGA Teaching and Club Professional Division, allows all of her beginning students to tee the ball up on every shot when they play on the course the first time. While using a tee is not legal on the course except when you are hitting your tee shot (the drive at the beginning of every hole), it is a great way to learn and build up your confidence.

Kerry had a funny experience with this approach. A company president came to her two weeks before a corporate golf outing to learn the game. He had never played golf before. Kerry worked with him four or five times before the outing. By the end he was feeling pretty good about the way he was hitting the ball.

Kerry suggested that he would have a more enjoyable time at the outing if he told his staff that he would play if they would let him use "beginner rules." They agreed, not knowing that meant he could tee up every shot.

So at the outing when he first got out a tee on the fairway, there were a few raised eyebrows. But no one said anything. After all, he was the president. After the round, though, everyone had a good laugh. They really liked "beginner rules" and so did he! They permitted him to join in the outing and have a good time with the more experienced golfers. And so can you as long as you're not competing against others who are playing according to the official USGA rules. So the first Ethics Check question—Is it legal?—can be dealt with by clarity about the rules being used.

"If something is legal, why would you need any other questions?" you may ask. Why not just go ahead and follow the rules? Because, sometimes in golf, particularly with a handicap system, something might be legal but it would not pass the second Ethics Check question—*Is it fair?* By that we mean, if you decide to do something, will it heavily favor one party over another so that there will clearly be a big winner or a big loser?

Let me give you some examples. My official handicap at the Skaneateles Country Club is 11, but I didn't play much last year. My back and kidney gave me problems and when I played, my scores were closer to a 16 handicap than an 11. At that time, for me to have played a match at an 11 would have been unfair to my partner and would not have reflected what the handicap system in golf is designed to accomplish—permit people of various abilities to compete against each other in a way that makes for a good match. So last summer I was clear with people about the reality of my game, and my partners and opponents renegotiated my handicap in our informal matches. As a result, we had some exciting matches. I certainly didn't play in any formal tournaments, though, where I was unable to renegotiate my handicap. This year, now that I am healthy again, I am playing a game consistent with my handicap.

Here's another example of a fairness situation. Jay Sigel, two-time U.S. amateur champion, British amateur champion, and the longest-standing member of the U.S. Walker Cup team, is a good friend. I caddied for Jay in the U.S. Junior Amateur Championship at Cornell University in 1961 when he was seventeen years old. I was twenty-one and had just graduated from Cornell. I was playing a lot at the time and knew the Cornell course like the back of my hand.

The U.S. Junior Amateur at that time was match play. Jay lost on the eighteenth hole in the final. We still have fun arguing whether he decided not to listen to me or I gave him the wrong club. At any rate, Jay hit his second shot into a greenside trap and lost the match.

Two weeks later Jay won the U.S. Junior Chamber of Commerce tournament in Denver (the second biggest junior amateur tournament) by eleven shots (it was a medal play tournament). He got a full scholarship to the University of Houston and then transferred to Wake Forest University in North Carolina. Early in his collegiate career at Wake Forest, Jay accidentally put his hand through a dormitory window. That ruined Jay's collegiate golf career and essentially his hopes of playing on the pro tour.

When Jay got the strength back in his hand and began to compete again, he decided to stay amateur. Today he is considered the greatest amateur golfer since Bobby Jones. As he looks back on his accident, Jay considers it a blessing, given his wonderful family, successful insurance business, and the fact that he can enjoy competitive golf at a high level without needing to win to build up his self-esteem.

That's all to set the stage for an example of fairness. Several years ago Jay was having another good run at the U.S. Amateur Championship. In a quarter-final match, he was leading another top amateur, Mitch Voges (who won the championship in 1991). Jay was 2 up with three holes to play. He had about a ten-foot putt for a par. Mitch had a four-foot putt. Jay asked him to mark his ball one club head to the right because the ball was in his line.

Jay putted and missed his putt. Voges put down his ball and was about to putt when Jay realized Voges had not replaced his ball to its original position. Rather than let Voges putt and have him called on an infraction (which would have resulted in an automatic loss of the hole and the match), Jay stopped him before he stroked the ball. Voges then replaced his ball appropriately, sank the putt to win the hole, and then went on to win the next two holes and the match.

The story of Jay's gesture was in the newspapers all over the country. Mitch Voges couldn't believe someone would do what Jay did. For Jay, the choice was easy. While he legally could have won the hole and the match, he decided he wouldn't like to win like that. It wasn't fair, he thought.

Fairness has to be decided by you and depends on your values and beliefs. Jay Sigel just doesn't need to win so badly that he would do something he thinks is unfair.

The Ethics Check question about fairness can also help people who make themselves and others miserable on the course. There are some rules against throwing clubs, but there is nothing illegal about arrogant or miserable behavior. Golfers need to realize that their behavior can and does have an impact on others. It is unfair to drag everyone else down to your level because you're having a bad round.

The final Ethics Check question stands alone as the most important. *How will it make you feel about yourself?* We already talked a little about this question when discussing *pride* and self-esteem in the last chapter. An unethical act will erode self-esteem. Questions like, "How would I feel if what I am considering doing was published in a local newspaper [or a club newsletter]?" or "Would I like my family and golfing friends to know?" also get at this issue. When it comes to what enhances and what distracts from your own feelings of esteem, the fact of the matter is:

*

There
Is
No
Right Way
to
Do
a
Wrong Thing.

*

I don't think golfers who have a poor memory, a good foot, or a lousy disposition would do some of the things they do if they knew that other people were aware of their shenanigans. Jay Sigel's decision to stop his opponent from breaking a rule was done as much from his solid self-esteem as from fairness. Jay is a great golfer; even so, he does not believe that who he is as a person is dependent upon whether he wins or loses a golf match. Many of us could learn from his example.

I live in a San Diego community called Rancho Bernardo that has a large retiree population. One morning my wife, Margie, and I were sitting with an older gentleman at a local breakfast spot, and he said an interesting thing: "If I knew when I retired how I felt about myself on any given day was going to be largely determined by how I played golf that day, I would have started the game a lot earlier in life."

Too many people, when they play, act like this man suggests he does: Who they are is what they score or how they play. So if they are not playing well, they may cheat or act badly. That's sad. There has to be more to life than golf. What we need to do is be more accepting of our golf game and less judgmental.

Remember the three Ethics Check questions; they can be a guide for helping you and others monitor your behavior and determine the right thing to do as you work toward goal accomplishment on the course.

PART TWO
GETTING BETTER AT GOLF

CHAPTER 3
Change: Why Is It Difficult to Learn New Habits?

Change is a highly personal experience. No two people react in exactly the same way. Some see it as danger; some see it as opportunity.

Once it is clear to you why you play golf—your *purpose*(s)—and what you want to accomplish with your golf game—your *goal*(s)—you may be ready to learn some new skills. If that is not the case, you may want to skip the next two chapters and move straight to the final part of the book, which is about application and commitment.

If you decide to learn some new skills, that may involve taking some lessons from a local teaching professional or going to a golf school or studying the game on your own by reading articles and books, viewing instructional videos, listening to audio programs on golf, or talking to more experienced players. No matter what method you choose, how do you know when you have learned something new? Learning takes place whenever a change in behavior or performance has occurred. So learning involves change.

One of the reasons most golfers don't improve after studying the game is that no one tells them how difficult it is going to be to change their behavior or performance. The implication is that if you go out and do what you are told, your improvement will be automatic. And yet, swinging differently, taking care of your physical well-being, or approaching your game with new mental and course management strategies are not easy. That's why one of the first things we teach students at our Golf University is to understand change.

There are three levels of change.[1] The first level is *knowledge*. This is where the easiest and least time-consuming change can be made. Just reading a good book or article or getting advice from a pro or a more experienced player can change your knowledge about some aspect of the game. The greater the commitment you make to improving your golf game, the more new knowledge you will acquire.

The second level of change involves *attitudes*. An attitude is an emotionally charged bit of knowledge. For example, through watching video clips of great players you can learn that they do not keep their head down after hitting the ball, and you can get excited to learn to let your head move naturally as you swing. You not only know something, but you feel positive about it.

While attitudes can drive you to want to change, they also tend to be harder to change than knowledge because of the old "Yes, but . . ." response. That's when people say, "I know what you're saying, *but* I'm not going to change my opinion." There was a woman at the Golf University who was a pretty good player but had always been told to keep her head down even after she had hit the ball and was beginning her follow-through. Having her head stuck looking at the ground stopped her weight shift to the left side on completion of the swing and lost a lot of power and distance for her. While she knew that what we were telling her was right, particularly when she viewed herself on video, she kept saying, "But I like the way I'm hitting the ball." We left her alone on that part of her game because we realized that unless she had a positive attitude toward what we were teaching, she would never change her behavior.

Behavior, the third level of change, is more difficult to change than either knowledge or attitudes. Why? Behavior is tougher to change because it's based on past habits; to change your habits you actually have to *do* something differently. New Year's resolutions are easy to make but hard to keep. Talk is cheap. It takes behavior to demonstrate a real change. We are all creatures of habit. That's why beginners are much easier to teach than experienced players—you don't have to "un-learn 'em." They have no bad habits. The time and difficulty it takes to change the way someone behaves or performs is a function of the size of that person's reservoir of past experience.

To illustrate this point, suppose I took an eyedropper full of red liquid and squeezed it three times into a glass of clear water. Would those three drops of red liquid change the color of the water in the glass? Yes! The water would take on a red tinge. What if I took those same three drops of red liquid and put them in a swimming pool. Would that change the color of the water in the pool? No! Why not? Because the size and volume of the water are too great for those red drops to change the overall color. Making significant changes in the behavior or performance of an experienced golfer will be more difficult than with a beginner. The reservoir of past experience for experienced players is much larger and thus they have more conditioned habit patterns.

Is it still possible to change the way you behave or perform if you are an experienced golfer? Sure! But you have to understand why it might be difficult to change some of your golf behavior and habits. On the opening night at the Golf University, we have our students experience a powerful activity that teaches them seven common reactions to change. In this chapter I want to share those common reactions with you. I feel the more you understand the reactions and resistances most people have to change, the easier it will actually be to improve and change something about *your own* golf game.

COMMON REACTIONS TO CHANGE

When people are first confronted with changing something they do, they tend to:

- *Feel awkward,* ill-at-ease, and self-conscious
- *Focus on what they have to give up,* not what they might gain
- *Feel alone* even if others are going through similar changes
- Be able to *handle only a few changes* at a time
- Display *different levels of readiness* to change
- Be concerned that they *don't have enough resources to change successfully*
- *Revert to old behaviors* if the pressure to change does not continue

First, *when people are confronted with change*, they often feel uncomfortable, awkward, silly, self-conscious, and even embarrassed—especially in the beginning. When this awkwardness occurs, most people tend to give up working on the change because they think they are doing it wrong. What you have to realize is that *awkwardness is natural when you are trying to change something*. In fact, if you don't feel awkward when you're trying something new, you're not doing anything differently. Let me give you a personal example.

When we first started the Golf University, I was a real "hooker"—not a happy hooker, but I tended to hit everything from right to left. One of our pros, Tom Wischmeyer, who is now our Director of Golf, said, "Ken, you have too strong a right-hand grip. Just turn your right hand a little bit to the left so you have a neutral grip."

When I did what Tom said, it felt so awkward that I couldn't imagine taking the club head back and ever getting it near the ball on the forward swing. But knowing that "awkwardness is natural," I said to Tom, "Stand back! This grip really feels awkward. I can't imagine where the shot will go." Since I also knew that what is awkward in the beginning will eventually feel natural if I do it often enough, I was willing to be persistent and use the grip he suggested. That was very helpful for me to know. Otherwise, I would have given up on the new grip the first time I encountered any difficulty. While it took me several weeks to be completely comfortable with my new grip, Tom was right and I am hooking the ball much less now.

Second, when *people are asked to change the way they do something*, their initial *focus* is *on what they have to give up* rather than on what they are going to gain. So often in a change effort, the "change agent" or teacher first focuses on the benefits to be derived from the change, and seldom gives the people being asked to change any time to *mourn the loss*.

At the Golf University we have crying towels on the range so people can cry and mourn the loss of old habits or ways of doing things that they might have liked but that are holding them back from getting better. They can mourn an old grip, stance, or way of chipping or putting the ball, or an old way of thinking or feeling. Unless they are permitted to mourn the loss, we find they "talk to themselves" and continue to resist new approaches. So, if you are working with a pro or studying the game on your own and you are given something new to try, get in touch with any loss you might feel before taking on the new change.

Third, *when people are asked to do something differently*, even if a lot of others are going through the same change, *they feel alone*. Why aren't New Year's resolutions more successful? Because when you announce a change you have in mind, important people in your life laugh and say, "I'll believe it when I see it" or "You said the same thing last year." To change or improve something, we need the support of others. The same is true with golf. If you want to improve your game, important people like your spouse, your partner, or your playing friends need to be on your side. In fact, you need to ask for their support.

If you want to improve how you play golf, it helps to play and practice with people who will encourage and cheer your efforts. It's hard enough to change something without having to do it all by yourself. To drive home the importance of support and help from others, I often tell the story about the man who was sleeping one night and an angel appeared at the end of his bed. She said, "Come with me. I want to show you the difference between heaven and hell." The man thought that would be fascinating, so he went.

When they got to hell, the angel took the man to a fabulous banquet with all kinds of food and drink. But as he looked around the room, he saw people moaning and groaning and crying. When he got closer, the man noticed that everyone had braces on their arms so they couldn't bend them to feed themselves. As a result, everyone was miserable in the midst of plenty.

Then the angel took the man to heaven. They went to a similar banquet, but when they entered the dining room the man saw everyone laughing, smiling, and having a wonderful time. And yet when he got closer, he could see that these people also had braces on their arms so they couldn't bend them to feed themselves. But in heaven they were picking up the food and feeding each other!

At the Golf University we do everything we can to encourage people to help each other and to find others back home who will help them. I remember one foursome that came to our school together. They played every Saturday and Sunday for years in an environment of fierce competition. After being at the Golf University, they decided to help one another rather than "ride" each other. Before a round they asked each other what score would please each person at the end of the round. In other words, each player set his or her own par. Then the rest of the foursome did everything they could to help that member reach his or her goal. They shared advice, cheered each other on, and the like. Whenever someone achieved or exceeded a goal, everyone would put money in a pot for a great end-of-the-season party. The more people in the foursome who succeeded, the better the party.

In working on your golf game, find people who will support you. That's why I recommend that you share this book with the friends, family, and professionals who are going to be on your golf improvement support team. If some of your old golfing buddies are not willing to support your new improvement program and still want to give you a hard time whenever possible, you might want to take a vacation from playing with them. When your golf game becomes solid at the new level, you may be ready again to handle their kidding.

Fourth, *when people are asked to change too much they can become overwhelmed and immobilized.* In fact, most people can handle only three or four changes at one time. Given more changes than that, people often go on "tilt"—they can't do anything well. That's a big problem with most golf schools and golf lessons. The pros may give you too many suggestions because they see many areas of potential improvement. Most people get "paralysis by analysis." As they stand over the ball, there are too many things to work on at the same time. They become immobilized.

During the first day at the Golf University, we analyze the mechanical aspect of our students' game through various methods, including a major emphasis on video feedback. At the end of the day, our pros sit with each of their students and set four or five learning goals—grip, address, putting stroke, etc., depending on ability. Once a student has agreed upon these goals, the pros do not point out additional areas of improvement in golf mechanics until the student demonstrates on the course and on the practice range that he or she has "graduated" in one of the agreed-upon goal areas. We know that if you can improve four or five aspects of someone's golf game, their performance and enjoyment of the game will soar.

During the second and third days of the program, as the students get more comfortable with their swing mechanics, we begin to set some goals for the physical and mental aspects of the game—remembering again to avoid overload. With some people we may even decide that focusing on their physical condition, like flexibility, or the way they mentally approach the game, like emotionalizing only the positive, might be more important for improvement than another mechanical solution.

Fifth, during a change effort, *people tend to display different levels of readiness to change.* The willingness to change creates progress. If you are ready and willing to commit to improve, you will. If you are reluctant or are playing at a comfortable level, you won't. Don't put yourself down; just know where you are.

Excellent teachers meet their students where they are. If someone at the Golf University is having difficulty with some change, we do not push that person. If we want our students to learn patience, we have to be patient with them.

Sixth, when a change effort starts, *people often are concerned that they don't have enough resources to make the changes.* They ask: "Are we going to get more resources? People, time, money . . . ?" What people want is the resources before they commit to change. My experience is that the commitment should come first and then the resources will follow.

That's exactly what happened to me with golf. I had not played much for fifteen years while our kids were growing up. After running around the country during 1982 and 1983 promoting *The One Minute Manager,* I was exhausted and my life was out of balance. I said to my wife, Margie, "I'm going to get back into golf. That always brought balance and perspective to my life when I was younger."

When I made a commitment to play golf well again, I did not know where I was going to find the time or who I could get to help me on my game. I just knew I was going to do it.

Shortly afterward, things started to happen. I got the call from Jerry Tarde, editor of *Golf Digest*, about working on "The One Minute Golfer" article. With that call, I was off to see Bob Toski, an invitation to the *Golf Digest* School followed, then I met Chuck Hogan, and on and on until the Golf University was founded in 1988. Now golf is a major part of my life. The resources are there if you have a clear vision about what you want to do and are committed to making it happen.

Seventh, and last, *if the pressure is taken off people who are attempting to change something, they will tend to revert back to their old behavior.* Do I have to say more about the need to follow up and develop a plan to manage your journey to better golf? I remember so well taking lessons and then trying to practice the changes. My efforts would work until I was away from the pro and playing against people I wanted to beat so badly I could taste it. Rather than trying my new grip or swing to cure my hook, I would just aim the shot two fairways to the right and bring it back. Pretty soon I was just back to my old game.

It is important for you to remember that *relapse is natural.* It's not the relapse itself that is the problem, it's what you do when a relapse occurs. That's why I encourage you periodically in this book to get back to your game plan—what you are working on. So often when we revert back to old behavior we give up on all we have learned. That's not to your advantage. So, no matter how many times you relapse, when it occurs, step back, take a deep breath, and get back to what you were working on. How many lessons or golf schools does it take to improve your game? Only the one you stick to!

CHAPTER 4
Instruction: How Do You Become Your Own Coach?

Golf is the most overtaught and least learned human
endeavor. If they taught sex the way they teach golf, the
race would have died out years ago.
—Jim Murray
Sports Columnist

Now that you understand why it is difficult to change your behavior and improve your performance, you are ready to begin your journey to better golf.

Some people manage their own journey right from the beginning. They are self-taught golfers. That's the way I first learned to play golf. I started by watching people play the game. Near my home where I grew up in New Rochelle, New York, was the Wykagyl Country Club. My family didn't belong to the club, but my friends and I used to sneak under the fence and watch people play. Later I got to do some caddying there.

Once a year a big tournament—the Palm Beach Round Robin—came to Wykagyl. All of the greats in those days came to play—Hogan and Snead, and Tommy Bolt, Jimmy Demaret, Roberto de Vicenzo from Argentina, Claude Harmon, Bobby Locke from South Africa, Lloyd Mangrum, "Porky" Oliver. You name them and they were there. Several summers when my dad was stationed in Washington, D.C., with the U.S. Navy, I got to watch a top-flight Ladies Professional Golf Association (LPGA) tournament in the District area. Legends like Patty Berg, Louise Suggs, and "Babe" Didrikson Zaharias were playing. When tournaments like these were on, I never missed a round. I became fascinated by the game right from the beginning.

I'll never forget the first time I went to a driving range. My father gave me a few pointers about how to grip the club and stand, and then I was off on a trial-and-error adventure. I would try something and then observe the results I got. If I liked the way I hit it, I would do it that way again. If I didn't, I would try a different approach.

Any time I could get a ride to the driving range I would. When I got older and bigger, I would beg my mother in the summers to take me to Saxon Woods or Maplemore—two public courses in Westchester County not far from my home. I played or hit balls whenever I got a chance, but I never had a lesson.

By the time I got to high school, I was playing in the low 80's and could beat most of my friends. When I made our high school golf team, I was thrilled because I thought I'd learn about the game. But my basketball coach, Paul Ryan, who was a fabulous guy, ended up being our golf coach—and he didn't know any more about the game of golf than I did. That's the way it was in the 1950's—golf instruction was in its infancy. That's why there are so many "strange" swings on the Senior Tour today and so few on the regular tours. No one ever told Miller Barber, Arnold Palmer, Chi Chi Rodriguez, or Lee Trevino they shouldn't swing the way they do. All they did was spend years experimenting and developing a swing that worked for them. In a recent *USA Today* article, Lee Trevino said, "If I can find a teacher who can beat me, maybe I'll take a lesson."

Lynn Marriott, director of the LPGA Training and director of the Playing School at our Golf University, often starts her sessions with LPGA teaching professionals by asking, "How many of you would like a swing that looks like Nancy Lopez's swing?"

Hardly anyone raises her hand. Then Lynn asks, "How many of you would like Nancy Lopez's bank account?" Everyone laughs! Obviously Nancy Lopez has spent a long time making her swing work for her.

Today, with "instant" everything, most people are not willing to become golf fanatics and practically live on the course in order to become good players. They want to shortcut hours on the practice range and years of playing to learn golf or improve their game quickly. That's why every year people all over America spend millions of dollars taking golf lessons, practicing on driving ranges, reading golf books and magazines, viewing golf videos, or attending golf schools. And yet, even with all that effort, I haven't met many people who improve as much as they would like.

Some of my friends who try to improve their score by studying the game often experience the "paralysis by analysis" mentioned earlier—they can hardly bring the club back because they are thinking so much about what they are doing with their stance, swing, follow-through, and so on. Has that ever happened to you? You decide you want to get better at golf and you actually get worse. I know that it has happened to me.

What I concluded was that most of the professionals teaching and writing about golf today know how to teach the mechanics of golf and can get you to hit well when they are there watching and directing you. What they haven't thought about as much is the transfer of the learning process—so you can continue to improve when you are playing on the course on your own.

In our article "The One Minute Golfer," Bob Toski was successful in turning over the learning process to the One Minute Manager by teaching him how to set clear goals, praise his own progress, and then redirect or reprimand less-than-desired performance. Was that a good idea? You'd better believe it! Unless you are able to operate independently on the course and manage your own journey, you will never be the kind of golfer you want to be. How can you learn to be a self-managed player? By receiving excellent instruction and coaching that teaches you important basics about golf and then helps prepare you to make that learning a permanent part of your game.

As I tell managers all the time in my seminars, the most important part of being an effective manager is not what happens when you are there, but what happens when you are not there. This is as true for golf teachers as it is for managers.

*

*It is
not
what happens
during
golf lessons
that counts
the most,
but
what happens to
students
afterward
when
they are
playing and
practicing
on their own.*

*

Effective teachers gradually change their teaching style so that the learner moves from dependency on the instructor to independence and self-monitoring. They seek to work themselves out of their jobs by preparing their students to own what they have learned and use it after the lesson is over. These teachers want you to go home bragging about how much *you* know about your golf game; not how much *they* know. This is where the relationship between management thinking and golf comes alive. For more than twenty-five years I have been teaching managers how to empower their people so that they can perform as well when their manager is not there as when he or she is present. Years ago this empowerment process was solely in the hands of the manager. Today it is a mutual responsibility between manager and staff or team. Why? Because everyone has access to the same information. Managers are no longer better educated than their people. More and more, with advanced information technology and increased vehicles of communication, everyone throughout an organization, if given the opportunity, not only seems to know what is going on, but what to do about it.

The same is true with teacher and student in golf. Today you both have access to the same information. You can read the same magazines and books, view the same videos, and attend similar seminars and clinics. As a result, if you decide you want to learn golf or improve your game through professional instruction, you must find a teacher who will work with you as a partner in the learning process. To help you and your teacher to become better partners, this chapter will discuss the dynamics of managing the journey from external direction and control by your teacher to internal direction and control by you—the student.

Is this important information for you to learn? I think so! Last year I met a man on a plane who was complaining about how much worse his golf game had gotten after a couple of lessons. I shared with him the concepts about empowerment that I will be presenting in this chapter. Then I suggested that he give his teaching pro another chance, but this time tell his instructor exactly what he wanted to happen at the lesson.

I ran into the same man a few months later at a convention. He remembered our conversation and came up to me after my speech. "I've really turned around my golf thanks to you."

I said, "How did I help?"

"By teaching me to coach our country club pro how to give me the kind of lesson I needed."

I asked, "What did you do?"

"I scheduled an hour lesson with him. I told him I wanted him to watch me hit a few balls and then suggest to me two or three things I could do differently in order to get the ball more 'airborne.' I had been hitting nothing but 'grounders' lately. By the end of the lesson I insisted I wanted to be able to hit a shot and tell whether I had done the things he had suggested and how to correct myself if I didn't."

"How did it go?" I wondered.

"Great!" he said. "The pro did exactly what I asked him to do and now I have a lot more fun playing. I've even gone back for some lessons on my short game and sand play with the same results."

"Did you give your instructor the same direction?" I asked.

"I sure did!"

While I think it is important for you to learn how golf teachers can empower their students, let me warn you that *the material in the rest of this chapter will be much more theoretical than the three previous chapters.* You may have to pay a little more attention, as if you were sitting next to me on a plane and I was in a teaching mood. Don't feel bad if you have to read some things over twice. If you become impatient or have decided to be a self-taught golfer, please feel free to skip this chapter and move on to the last part of the book to learn how you would behave if you *were* a self-managed player. Later on, after you have finished the rest of the book, you might want to return to this chapter.

How to Begin the Journey

Before beginning a golf improvement program, the first thing you need to develop with your teacher are some SMART learning goals in the areas you need to concentrate on. At the end of the first day at the Golf University, each student sits down with his or her instructor and sets four to five SMART learning goals for his or her three- or four-day stay with us. While our students learn some aspects of the game outside their goal areas, the focus of learning is centered around becoming their own coach in those established areas. *We have learned that to get better at golf, all you have to learn is a few new things or correct a few bad habits.* Remember the 80/20 rule. Eighty percent of the improvement you want from golf will come from only 20 percent of the things you need to learn or improve. Good teachers focus on only a few key areas. This does not mean that the game of golf is simple. It just means that for you to play and enjoy it you just need regularly to remember and use a few basics. To drive a car you don't have to know everything about the motor. All you need to know is how to turn on the motor, step on the gas, apply the brakes, and steer the car.

Peter Thomson, five-time winner of the British Open, put it well when he suggested, "To play good golf all you have to do is grip it, turn it, and release it." At the Golf University we translate that into (1) getting in a good athletic address position—proper grip, stance, and posture; (2) turning away from the ball on the backswing in a way that stores up energy; and (3) releasing that energy with a good forward swing that sends the ball to the target. Variations of those three basics apply to every shot whether it be a putt, chip, sand shot, pitch, or full swing with an iron or a wood.

Once your goals are set, you are ready to start the journey to becoming *your own coach*. To help you and your instructor get started, let me describe four steps that have to be followed to teach anybody anything. These steps are grounded in the three management secrets that Spencer Johnson and I wrote about in *The One Minute Manager*—One Minute Goal Setting, One Minute Praisings, and One Minute Reprimands and Redirection.[1] While they are initially teacher dominated, gradually over time, with you and your instructor working together, these four steps should become student dominated.

*

FOUR BASIC TEACHING STEPS

1. Clarify the task to be performed.
2. Let the student do it.
3. Observe the student's performance.
4. Praise the student's progress and/or redirect his or her efforts.

*

If you were to observe any outstanding instructor teaching a new skill to someone, you would see these teaching steps in action.

1. *Clarify the task to be performed.* This is accomplished in three ways: verbally, visually, and kinesthetically.

    - *Tell*—Tell the person what to do and why. For example, your teacher might say:
      "I want you to start your swing with upper body rotation, not your hands and arms. A swing that starts with upper body rotation will have more power."

    - *Show*—Another way to clarify the task is to show the person how to do it. Now your teacher might demonstrate a swing that starts with upper body rotation or show a good video example of the swing.

    - *Experience*—Finally, your instructor may prescribe a drill that will allow you as a student to *feel* the new technique: That's what "kinesthetic" learning is all about. For example, he or she might suggest that you take a swing or two with your feet together. This would force you to start your swing with the upper body and give you an opportunity to experience how that feels.

Clarifying the task to be performed is all about One Minute Goal Setting. As we have said over and over, all good performance starts with clear goals.

2. *Let the student do it.* After your teacher has clarified the task to be performed, the second step involves having you do the prescribed task. Kathy Dougherty, one of the top instructors at the Golf University, calls this step "Nike Golf—just do it!" Your teacher might say:
"Let me see a swing that starts with upper body rotation."
Now your instructor cuts back on teacher direction and begins to turn the direction for performance over to you as a student. This is a familiar aspect of all golf instruction—whether or not the time has been taken to isolate specific goals.

3. *Observe the student's performance.* This is a key step if learning is to take place. Why should you and/ or your teacher observe your performance? So that initially your instructor, and eventually you, can do the fourth and most important step.

4. *Praise the student's progress and/or redirect his or her efforts.* This is where One Minute Praising, Redirection, and an occasional One Minute Reprimand come into play. First, let me emphasize that helping golfers to improve requires praising. I bet you like a pat on the back when you are learning. However, the word "progress" is key here. If your teacher waits to praise you as a student until you demonstrate perfect behavior, your teacher may wait forever. In other words, it is almost impossible to do something exactly right in the beginning. We all learn a little bit at a time. As a result, if your pro wants you to modify your swing, your teacher should praise the slightest progress you make in the desired direction. Remember:

*

*Anything
worth
doing
does not
have
to
be done
perfectly
at
first.*

*

Many parents use this process of praising *progress* without really being aware of it. For example, suppose you want to teach your daughter to say, "Please give me a glass of water," but she has never spoken before. You would have a dead (dehydrated) child if you waited for her to say that full sentence before giving her any water. It would also not be helpful to yell at or punish your daughter for not doing what she doesn't know how to do. She does not have a clue how to speak. To teach her to say, "Please give me a glass of water," you would probably start with the word "water." You would say the word "water" over and over again to demonstrate what you want your daughter to say. Finally, one day when she says "laler"—something that sounds like "water"—you go wild. You get grandmother on the phone to show off your daughter's progress and you hug and kiss her. Now that wasn't "water" but it wasn't bad—it was progress. Since you don't want your daughter going into restaurants at age twenty-one asking for a glass of "laler," after a while you decide to accept only "water" and then move on to "please" and other words. When you use this typical pattern in teaching a child to speak, whether you know it or not, you are praising your child for small accomplishments as he or she moves closer and closer to the desired behavior of talking and saying, "Please give me a glass of water."

When one of our students hits a shot early in the program at the Golf University or takes a practice swing that is in the direction of the desired change, our instructors accent the positive. They look for something that is praiseworthy.

> *"You transferred your weight to the left side well as you moved into the ball"* or *"You were in a good athletic position at address with your weight on the balls of your feet."*

Then, if improvement is still possible, our instructors will move to the second half of the fourth step—redirect. It is important to distinguish between "**and** redirect" and "**or** redirect."

The "and redirect" means that when someone is learning how to do something, after you've praised his or her progress, it is appropriate then to redirect and give that person some more information that will make the next attempt even better. For example:

> *"With the next swing, see if you can get a fuller shoulder turn."*

The "or redirect" means that if you've observed something and there is no progress, go straight to redirect. As a teacher, you assume the responsibility for poor performance. You might say:

> *"Maybe I didn't make it clear enough. Let me try to explain what I'd like you to do in a different way."*

Nowhere in these four steps is there any mention of the One Minute Reprimand. When you are in a learning mode, any form of negative feedback could immobilize you. The only place for a reprimand is when you have been doing something well for a period of time and now suddenly are getting sloppy or careless and not doing what you already know how to do. Then a reprimand from your teacher would tell you what you did wrong, how it made him or her feel (disappointed, frustrated, and so on), and then reaffirm your ability to perform well again in that area.

> *"You had very little weight shift on the last few shots. You hit every shot almost completely with your hands and arms. I'm disappointed because I've been watching you do it right all during the lesson. I know you can get back on track with your weight shift."*

In summary, when you are first attempting to become a self-managed player, your instructor, with your support, must direct the four teaching steps. That is, he or she must (1) *clarify the task* to be performed; then (2) *let you do it;* (3) *observe your performance;* and finally, (4) *praise any progress* in the desired direction *and/or redirect your efforts.* This process should continue until you, the student, can eventually do all the steps yourself.

When *you* are able to determine what to do with something you have been learning, and then do it and self-monitor your performance, your teacher has guided you from dependence to independence. Now the learning process has moved from teacher-dominated learning to student-dominated learning.

Managing the Journey

What prevents golfers from becoming independent of their teacher is that they, as well as their instructor, don't have a clear picture of what the journey from dependence to independence looks like. At the Golf University, our teaching professionals use Situational Leadership (SL II®)[2] to visualize this journey as a railroad track with four stops (teaching stations) moving from *Directing,* to *Coaching,* to *Supporting,* and, finally, to *Delegating.* These four teaching stations differ in three ways: (1) the amount of direction the teacher provides, (2) the amount of support the teacher provides, and (3) the amount of student involvement in the learning process.

Situational Leadership: Four Teaching Stations

FIRST STOP: STYLE 1—DIRECTING—The Instructor:

TEACHER
DOMINATED

- Clarifies the task to be performed
- Develops action plan for student
- Provides specific direction
- Supervises and evaluates student performance

SECOND STOP: STYLE 2—COACHING—The Instructor:

SOME
STUDENT
INVOLVEMENT

- Clarifies the task to be performed
- Develops action plan but consults student
- Explains what needs to be done but solicits ideas from student
- Continues to supervise and evaluate student performance

THIRD STOP: STYLE 3—SUPPORTING—The Instructor:

SOME
TEACHER
INVOLVEMENT

- Involves student in problem identification and goal setting
- Asks the student how the task is to be done
- Listens to and facilitates student's problem solving and decision making
- Works with student to evaluate student performance

FOURTH STOP: STYLE 4—DELEGATING—The Instructor:

STUDENT
DOMINATED

- Defines problems with student and sets goals collaboratively
- Allows student to develop own action plan
- Only periodically monitors student performance
- Allows student to evaluate own performance

According to Situational Leadership, there is *no one best teaching approach*. It all depends on your development level—your skill and confidence level in whatever you are trying to learn or improve. Each of the stops or teaching stations is appropriate for a corresponding level of learner development. If your development level for something you want to learn is:

- Development Level 1, you are an *"enthusiastic beginner"*—someone who has confidence that he or she can learn but lacks any real skill and, therefore, needs to be told what to do—a *Directing* (S1) style is best for you.
- Development Level 2, you are a *"disillusioned learner"* —someone who has some skills but may be discouraged and, therefore, needs both direction and support—a *Coaching* (S2) style is most suitable.
- Development Level 3, you are a *"cautious performer"*—someone who has the necessary knowledge and skill to perform but lacks confidence to do it on his or her own and, therefore, needs to be listened to and encouraged—a *Supporting* (S3) style will help you the most.
- Development Level 4, you are a *"self-managed player"*—someone who has the skills and confidence to self-monitor his or her own behavior and, therefore, needs little direction or support from a teacher—a *Delegating* (S4) style is the right approach.

If a teacher wants to go from a *Directing* style (Station 1) that is most helpful to a beginner, to a *Delegating* style (Station 4) that fits a player who has the necessary skill and confidence to perform well without supervision, what two stations does the teacher have to go through first? The answer is, quite obviously, *Coaching* (Station 2) and *Supporting* (Station 3), so as to help the student work through any disillusionment or cautiousness that may occur.

The problem I have found is that most golf teachers do not "stay on the tracks" from one station to the next and get "derailed" by moving from a *Directing* style, where they are clarifying the task to be performed and monitoring your performance with little input from you, to a *Delegating* style, where they say, "Good luck." This sets you up to fail, since the teacher has not moved you along the tracks appropriately so that new learnings can be applied immediately. You are sent off on your own too soon. What you need to do is find a teacher who will stay on the tracks with you as he or she guides you to the final destination—independence and the capacity to do on your own what you have learned.

Let me give you a personal example to illustrate the power of on-track teaching behavior and how someone can move over time from being a dependent learner to a self-managed player. At age seventeen, my daughter Debbie decided that she wanted to learn to play golf; so I made an appointment for her with a local pro. Since Debbie was an *enthusiastic beginner*, she didn't know what to expect and, therefore, didn't care whether the pro asked her any questions or patted her on the back. The only thing she was concerned about was getting basic information on how to grip the club, stand, and swing. The pro obliged and started at the *Directing* (S1) station, spending most of his time clarifying the fundamentals that Debbie had to learn, like grip, stance, posture, backswing, and forward swing, and then observing her doing each of the fundamentals and providing appropriate feedback.

The assumption was that Debbie had an "empty barrel" of knowledge and experience, and therefore it was the job of the instructor to fill up her barrel. *Directing* is thus a "barrel filling" style. The teacher is giving information and the student is listening and attempting to do as told.

After several lessons, *disillusionment* started to set in with Debbie. She broke a few nails and began to get some calluses on her hands. She started to tell her mom things like, "I don't think golf is for me," and, "This is harder than I expected." Such responses are natural. After the honeymoon period is over, reality sets in. And reality says it is usually a lot harder to get to the level of skill you'd like to be than you thought. Golfers need patience and persistence to improve. How severe the disillusionment becomes depends on how quickly your teacher moves from the *Directing* (S1) station to the *Coaching* (S2) station.

So I called up the pro and said, "Disillusionment is setting in with Debbie." (I had taught Situational Leadership to most of the staff at the club.) "Why don't you call her and make a date to have a Coke with her and see if you can get her to take another lesson. Debbie needs some encouragement now in addition to technical direction."

It is at this point that most golf professionals and schools get off the tracks. When disillusionment sets in they are nowhere to be found. The local pro would have just wondered why Debbie stopped taking lessons. The teaching process got derailed: The teacher went from a *Directing* style (Station 1) to a *Delegating* style (Station 4) and never stopped at *Coaching* or *Supporting* (Stations 2 and 3). The chances that any student can leave the first level of development and move to the fourth and last stop without assistance are next to nothing.

In Debbie's case, the local pro did move his style to the *Coaching* station and provided support as well as direction; he was able to coach Debbie through the disillusionment stage. During this time at the *Coaching* station, he not only continued to give Debbie new information, but he made sure he answered all her questions and praised and encouraged her progress. While the teacher was still in charge of direction, communication was now more two-way between Debbie and the pro. This style involves both "barrel filling" and "barrel drawing out," that is, drawing upon the experiences Debbie already had. When Debbie finally started to hit the ball pretty well off the practice tee, the pro said, "Debbie, I think you're ready to go on the course and play."

"Great!" she said, "When are we going?"

"I'm not going," he said.

"What do you mean, you're not going?" asked Debbie. "I'm not going out there by myself. Do you want me to make a fool of myself?"

Why did Debbie need the pro with her on the course? To tell her what to do? No. She just needed some support to get over her lack of confidence about performing on her own and transferring her new skills to a new situation: playing on the golf course. Most teaching pros don't usually consider having a "playing lesson" with beginners. They usually reserve those lessons for "good" players. And yet beginners need playing lessons much more than experienced players. Even teachers who move from *Directing* (Station 1) to *Coaching* (Station 2) tend to go straight to *Delegating* (Station 4), from giving encouragement and advice to having their students provide those things all on their own. Yet once again, there are no tracks between the *Coaching* and *Delegating* stations. The pro has to move first to *Supporting* (Station 3) before the students are ready to be out on the course alone as self-managed players.

The assumption with a *Supporting* style is that you, the student, come to the task with a fairly "full barrel" of knowledge and experience, but are cautious and lack confidence to apply and consistently use that knowledge on your own. Therefore, it is the job of your teacher to draw on your barrel of experience, and reinforce what you already know to be correct until it is an incorporated part of your behavior. *Supporting* is thus a "barrel drawing out" style. Your teacher listens, facilitates, and encourages you to trust and own what you already know.

Some pros may not be comfortable with this station because they are not providing any new information to students but instead are simply observing and reminding them about what they have already been told. Many pros feel that time spent just providing praise is unnecessary and something that students should be able to do on their own. Such an attitude however, is a *big* mistake, and a lot of potential learning is never given a chance to become a habit because the student lacks self-confidence.

So I asked the pro to give Debbie a couple of playing lessons during which he operated at the *Supporting* station: He did not give Debbie any new information, but worked with what she already knew. His main role was to support and encourage her and to reach into her barrel of knowledge to help her find answers to any problems or questions.

After the second playing lesson, Debbie came home and said to me, "Dad, would you like to play some golf tomorrow?"

I was thrilled because I knew that her instructor, with some prodding by me, had gradually moved Debbie from *Directing* (Station 1), where he had to provide all the direction and feedback, through *Coaching* and *Supporting* (Stations 2 and 3) until she had built up enough confidence to be willing and able to progress to *Delegating* (Station 4) and play with me and her friends. It meant she had overcome any disillusionment and cautiousness that she had felt toward golf and had developed from an enthusiastic beginner to a self-managed player.

Now, was Debbie a tournament player just because the pro could use a delegating style with her? No. But she had progressed enough so she could go out and enjoy the game. She could stand behind the ball and decide what she wanted to do with a particular shot, and then do it. After hitting the shot, she could observe the results, pat herself on the back for whatever was praiseworthy, and then redirect her efforts, if necessary, for the next time she had a chance to hit that kind of shot. In other words, she could manage herself around the course.

While I had to prod Debbie's instructor to stay on the tracks, you can do the same with your instructor now that you understand Situational Leadership and what it takes to manage your journey from dependence to independence. Just like the man I met on the plane, you can help your instructor to give you the kind of lessons you need.

While your teacher should give you a lot of direction in the beginning of a lesson at the *Directing* (S1) station, once a learning goal has been set, make sure that your teacher doesn't spend the whole lesson giving you "information overload"—telling you everything he or she ever knew about the subject. As soon as possible, the teacher needs to move to the *Coaching* (S2) station to permit you to ask all kinds of questions as well as provide you with needed encouragement. The next stop is at the *Supporting* (S3) station, where your teacher begins to switch roles and ask you to provide information: "How did the shot feel?" "What went wrong or poorly?" "What are you going to try to do on the next shot?" And finally, when the lesson nears its conclusion, you know enough about what your teacher was trying to teach you to be able to self-praise when things go well and self-correct when things go wrong: *Delegating* (S4). If your pro manages this journey correctly, your development level will gradually move from an enthusiastic beginner to a self-managed player. Then you will be able to become your own coach.

After Debbie plays enough using what she has learned, she may want to get even better. There are a number of students at the Golf University who have attended the school several times. Each time they return, a new set of learning goals is set with their instructor that will move them down the road to even better golf.

Whenever you return for further instruction, your teacher, according to Situational Leadership, should *move back one station* to a *Supporting* (S3) style from the *Delegating* (S4) station that ended the last interaction. For example, Debbie's teacher might start any new instruction by asking her how she had been playing and what she thought would help her move to another playing level. When he got a sense of where Debbie was with her golf, the pro could then move back one more stop to the *Coaching* (S2) station and begin to provide direction and support to help her begin the journey again to independence. Once you have worked with a teacher and gained some independence, there is probably no reason for that teacher ever to move back along the railroad tracks to the original *Directing* (S1) station. But remember, it is just as important for your instructor to stay on the tracks when moving back to deal with a new need as it is in moving forward to build independence.

The example with Debbie was meant to give you a big picture of how the journey from dependence to independence has to be managed. However, I need to correct any impression you might have received that development level is a global concept—that people are at a single development level for their total golf game. On the contrary, *development level is a task-specific concept.* During the same period of time, you may be at all four development levels for different aspects of your game. For example, you may be a self-managed learner when it comes to putting, a cautious performer with your woods, a disillusioned learner with your sand play, and an enthusiastic beginner with your course management. You may need a different teaching style for whatever part of your game you are working on. There is no stigma to any development level; each one merely signals where you are in that learning area and what should be the appropriate initial teaching station for an instructor.

The teaching-learning process does not always start at the *Directing* (S1) station. You may seek instruction when you are disillusioned about something you have been trying to do and may initially need a coaching style; or if you have lost confidence about something you had been doing successfully and now need an instructor to start at the *Supporting* (S3) station. *No matter at which teaching station you start, you and your instructor have always to realize that when the lesson is over, your teacher is forced to go to the* Delegating *(leave alone) teaching station.* Given that reality, your teacher must strive (and you must demand that he or she strive) to move you along gradually to becoming your own coach, to progress from a teacher-controlled to a student-controlled learning style. During every lesson, your teacher must gradually work him or herself out of a job and place the responsibility for learning and improvement on you as a student.

PART THREE

MAINTAINING YOUR PROGRESS

CHAPTER 5
Application: How Do You Use What You've Learned?

The essence of knowledge is, having it, to use it.
—Confucius

As I indicated in the previous chapter, the ultimate test of a golf lesson or golf school is not what happens when you are being guided and observed by pros, but what happens afterward when you are on your own: on the practice tee or on the course without the benefit of a teacher's presence. If you have helped your teacher guide you from dependence to independence, you have become a self-managed player. What does that mean? That's what this chapter is all about.

Preparing to Play

Most weekend or occasional golfers don't do much to prepare to play. The only thing they really worry about is making sure they get to the course before their designated tee-off time. I'm always amazed at the number of golfers who leave hardly any time to warm up mentally or physically before starting a round of golf. Sometimes you see them tying their shoes on the first tee. That seldom happens in other sports.

In an ideal world it would be best to head out to the course at a leisurely pace, arriving about an hour before you are scheduled to play. On the way out to the course, *you need some way to transition from what you have been doing to the task at hand—playing and enjoying a round of golf.* I consider it a blessing that my car phone doesn't work on my way to the two courses I play the most—Pauma Valley Country Club in southern California and Skaneateles Country Club in upstate New York. On my way to both courses, I have to pass through beautiful, remote countryside. If I put the top down on my car, play some soothing music, and begin to soak in the beauty of the surroundings, by the time I arrive I am mellow and have done a good job of setting the stage for an enjoyable round of golf. If I'm late, as is sometimes the case, all my attention and energy is focused on getting to the course as quickly as possible. In talking to golfers ranging from tour players to high handicappers, I have found that everyone seems to agree that racing into a round of golf is not a good idea.

What do you do when you get to the course? The first thing you might want to *do* is *some stretching exercises*. At the Golf University, we teach our students a stretching program that combines some of the yoga-type exercises that characterize the Egosque method with the work of Dr. Frank Jobe. Peter Egosque, who is credited with extending Jack Nicklaus's golfing career, has a new book entitled *The Egosque Method* that tells us about his wonderful approach to physical well-being. Jobes's pioneering work in designing exercises especially for golfers is contained in *Thirty Exercises to Better Golf*.

Does stretching before a round help? Absolutely! Tom Wischmeyer, Director of Golf at the Golf University, conducted an interesting experiment for six months with his own game. Instead of hitting full swing practice shots before a round (he did do some chipping and putting), he did twenty minutes of stretching exercises. He found that this routine prepared him for the first few holes as well as, or even better than, hitting balls on the range. For me, some stretching is a must before a round, particularly as I get older or the course I am playing has no practice range.

If you do hit balls, which is by no means a bad idea, the intent should be to loosen up, not to work on swing mechanics. Right before a round is not the time to revamp your swing. You have to go with what you "brought to the dance." At the Golf University, we recommend that you *start through your bag backward*. First, hit a few chips and putts and slowly move from your wedge up to your driver. It's good to complete your loosening-up routine with your driver, or whatever you hit off the tee, because that will be the first club you use on the course.

Remember to practice as close to game conditions as possible. That means going through your entire routine for each practice shot: stepping away from the ball, picking a target, selecting a club, and preparing to hit the ball; then approaching the ball and hitting it; and finally observing and analyzing the results. When most people practice, they put the range balls in a position where they can easily "rake them in" and hit shots in "rapid-fire succession" without moving their position from the last shot. We'll talk about your pre-shot, swing, and post-shot routines later in the chapter.

While you are getting into the rhythm of the game on the range, it might be a good time to *review why you play golf.* Is it for fun, camaraderie, beauty, or for the competition? Make sure you don't forget about your purpose(s). No matter what happens on the course, you need to keep your reasons for playing golf paramount. Otherwise, you may let your results determine whether you enjoy the round or not.

Setting Realistic Goals

As I have implied several times, it does not make sense for you to play against the course par of 70 to 72 unless you are a zero or scratch handicap. (That means you normally shoot par.) As a result, I have developed a *goal-setting system* that seems to help people compete against their own par. Here is how it works:

After loosening up, get a scorecard from the course and begin to set your own par. Given how you are feeling, how you have been playing lately, the condition of the course, and the weather, what score would please you to have shot if we were sitting in the clubhouse having a drink after the round? In other words, what is your hoped-for score? Suppose that score was 89. If the course par was 72, that would mean you would need to shoot at least a 45 on one nine and a 44 on the other. In terms of the regular par, *your par* would be 17 bogeys and 1 par. But you can set up your own par any way you want.

Suppose you tend to start slow and finish strong. You might want to set your par on the first hole at 6 if it is a par 4. Now, if you get a 5 on the first hole when your par was 6, it is a psychological lift to be able to go to the second tee 1 under par rather than 1 over. You could set par for yourself on a given hole at any amount as long as your total ends up to your hoped-for goal of 89. Once you start to shoot consistently below that goal, you could lower your goal to 87 and begin to stretch yourself again. With this system you are being very specific and giving yourself a goal to shoot at not only for the entire round but also for each hole, a goal that might be more realistic than the course-designated par.

Monitoring Your Play

This scoring system is taught at the Golf University and has helped a number of people enjoy the game more and accomplish the results they desire. For example, former top NFL official Jim Tunney came to the Golf University last year. Now that Jim is retired, he is taking up the game. I played nine holes with him and made him a believer in the scoring system.

Jim set his par at 55 before we teed off the first hole. Since the par at the Pala Mesa Resort course where we played is 36 for the first nine, Jim could have 8 double bogeys and 1 triple bogey to reach his own par. On the first hole, a par 5 up the hill, Jim set his par at 7. He hit a good drive and second shot, setting himself up for a possible sub-par hole. But his third shot landed in a greenside bunker and he took 3 to get out and got an 8 on the hole. Rather than going to the second tee with a triple bogey, he had a bogey. He wrote +1 on his card. In this scoring system, you don't write down your score; only how many shots you were under or over your par.

On the second hole, Jim hit his first drive out of bounds and got another 8, but this time on a par 4. Since his par was 6, Jim had a 2 over par double bogey. On the third hole, another par 5, Jim had some more difficulties and another 8. But after three 8's in a row, he was only 4 over *his* par.

The 4th hole is the Number One handicap hole on the course, so Jim's par was a 7 on this long par 4. He hit a great drive and got on the green in 3. He came alive like a kid as he was putting for a double eagle 4. He just missed the putt, but settled for a 2 under par eagle. When you only play against the course's par, you might never have a chance for an eagle in your whole life.

Jim now went to the par 3 next hole only 2 over par. This got his competitive spirit going. When he got a birdie 4, he was now only 1 over par. Over the last four holes, Jim made up that stroke and finished his nine-hole round with an even par 55. Jim was thrilled. As we sat in the clubhouse having a soft drink, he said, "Any other day if I had started off with three 8's in a row I would have been psychologically destroyed and probably would have had a bad round. But with setting my own par I felt like I was always in the game."

To help people use this scoring system and better monitor their playing, Michael O'Connor and I developed (with feedback from the Golf University staff) a special scorecard that allows you to set your own goals, track your progress toward them, and discover what areas of your game you need to practice.

	HOLE	1	2	3	4	5	6	7	8	9	OUT	FRONT NINE SUMMARY
RESULTS	COURSE PAR											
	− PERSONAL PAR											Praisings (What went well?)
	+ OR − YOUR PAR											
	Good Shots—Mark Each With A Plus Sign (+)											
REASONS	TEE SHOTS											
	FAIRWAY SHOTS											Redirections (What to do differently on the back nine?)
	SHORT SHOTS											
	PUTTS											
	SELF-MANAGEMENT											
	HOLE	10	11	12	13	14	15	16	17	18	IN	TOTAL
RESULTS	COURSE PAR											
	PERSONAL PAR											
	+ OR − YOUR PAR											
	Good Shots—Mark Each With A Plus Sign (+)											
REASONS	TEE SHOTS											
	FAIRWAY SHOTS											
	SHORT SHOTS											
	PUTTS											
	SELF-MANAGEMENT											

The Golf University Scorecard

As you will notice on the card, the first three rows of boxes are for monitoring *results* on each hole, using the scoring system I have been describing. In the first row, you write down the *course par* for each of the 18 holes. In the next row, you put down your own *personal par.* Remember, I said that if you normally shoot a 90 and the par is 72, that is 18 over par, so your par for each hole could be a bogey. You fill in your personal par accordingly. After each hole, you indicate in the third row whether you were over, under, or even with par. If you were over or under your par, how many? You do not put down your actual score. Write down, for example, $+1$ or $+2$. As my experience with Jim Tunney suggests, a high number is much more discouraging than how many over par you scored. The same is true for sub-par scores. It is much more motivating to see a -1 or -2 than the actual score.

The first four rows after *reasons* are for analyzing and keeping track of each of your shots—tee shots, fairway shots, short shots, and putts. Note that we ask you only to keep track of good shots and mark each with a plus $(+)$. Writing a minus $(-)$ is not allowed. We want you *only* to catch yourself doing things right! Why? As Chuck Hogan continually emphasizes, if you emotionalize only the good, you can create a reference library in your mind filled with only good experiences. So, if you hit a good tee shot, put a plus $(+)$ in that box. If you follow that with a good 4-iron, write $+4$; if it was a good 3-wood, write $+3W$. If you miss-hit a pitching wedge, don't be emotional and don't write anything in the short-shot box for that hole. Accent only the positive. Chuck Hogan and David Witt emphasize this way of managing your emotions:

*

*Without emotion
my bad shot
will fade
in my memory.*

*With emotion,
my good shots
shall be highlighted
for future use.*

*In this way
I shall create
the experience of
a champion.*

—Chuck Hogan and David Witt
*Playing the Game:
A Handbook for Golfers*

*

Most good players don't show much emotion when they hit a bad shot. For example, when Jay Sigel hits a bad shot, he assumes it is a complete accident and won't happen again, so he gives it very little emotion.

If you've ever watched Jay play in the Walker Cup or any of the great amateur events, you might say, "That's nothing new. Jay Sigel never shows any emotion at all. You can never tell from his face or appearance whether he's playing well or not."

I asked Jay about that. He told me he had always prided himself on keeping his emotions under control. But he did say, "When I hit a good shot I tell myself, 'Good shot' and then respond with an inner smile. On the outside you wouldn't notice but there is a difference in the way I respond to a well-struck shot and a poor one."

Jack Nicklaus can tell you every important shot he has ever hit in his career. But can he tell you the bad ones? I read that one day someone asked Jack how to cure a shank at a clinic he was conducting. Jack said, "I don't know. I've never hit one!"

With that response, another person in the audience shouted out, "That's not true, Jack." Then the person went on to remind Jack about the time during a major tournament when he hit a shank.

Jack quickly responded, "I don't remember that shot. Next question!"

Do I need to say more about accenting the positive!

At the end of both your front nine (first nine holes) and your entire eighteen-hole round, examine where your pluses fall. Are they bunched in one area like putting or are they spread out over several areas? Ask yourself: Where do I need more good shots? The answer to that question will suggest areas for redirection for the back nine as well as areas for future practice and learnings after your round. But remember, don't be too hard on yourself. Jay Sigel feels that the real fascination with golf comes from "the challenge of hitting the perfect shot, and yet you may only hit two or three a round."

The last *reason* row is for self-management. In this row you are given an opportunity to analyze two things: (1) your course management (how well you think you stuck to a sensible game plan as you played the hole) and (2) your emotional management (how well you think you used your emotions and feelings as a positive factor in your performance). Again, you are asked only to record the positive self-management experiences. Let's look at some examples.

How did you do on course management? If you hit a bad shot and then you tried to make it all up on the next shot but got yourself in worse trouble, that's poor course management. Don't write anything down for that hole in the self-management row. The rule about trouble is, only waste one stroke on it if at all possible. When in doubt, get your ball back on the fairway in play. If you hit your drive in the woods and played it back on the fairway and got a bogey, that's good course management. Write down a +CM (course management) in the self-management row for that hole.

How about emotional management? Did you let your anger over one bad shot cost you more strokes? If you made a costly mistake but kept your emotions under control, that might be good emotional management for you. Or if you let your emotions out (you could never be a Jay Sigel) and expressed your anger but managed to get back to business right away, that might be good emotional management for you. In either case, you would write down a +EM (emotional management) in the self-management box for that hole. Some people act like they're on emotional roller coasters and their golf game shows it. If everything is going well, they are on top of the world; but if things go sour, their emotions can keep them down. The management of your emotions is an important ingredient in making golf more fun and in accomplishing the results you desire.

Some people find filling out the card during a round is distracting, so they wait until they are at the nineteenth hole. Since you are asked only to recall the positive, that should be an easy task. And isn't that the best way to spend your time at the nineteenth hole—patting yourself on the back for all the good things you did?

If the scorecard I am suggesting here is not to your liking, you can create your own card. Then you can keep track of the things you think are important about your playing of golf. By using a scorecard to monitor your play, this postgame analysis can be very helpful for praising any progress and in redirecting your efforts where appropriate. When that happens, you really have become your own coach. Let me explain this in more detail.

Golf is played one shot at a time. Players who manage themselves well realize this and try to make the most out of each shot. In doing that, these golfers, in their own unique ways, are able to work through the four teaching steps discussed in the previous chapter by themselves. In your own golf game, that would mean, for any given shot you could: (1) decide what to do; (2) do it; (3) observe what you did; and then (4) praise whatever is praiseworthy and/or redirect future efforts. In other words, you become your own teacher. In talking further about coaching yourself, I will divide the discussion into the three aspects of every shot: Pre-shot routine, swing routine, and post-shot routine.

Pre-shot Routine

The *first decision* you have to make before you hit a golf shot is *what club are you going to use.* How do you select the appropriate one? You have to ask yourself some questions: How far away am I from my target? Even if you are not close enough to the green to aim at the pin, you should always aim at a target. If you hit this shot well, where do you want it to land?

In addition to distance, ask yourself about the playing environment—the wind, the condition of the ground, and the elevation. Is the wind with you or against you? Is the ground wet or dry? Are you shooting uphill or downhill to your target? As a result, should you use more or less club than usual for a shot of that distance?

How are you dressed? Are you wearing a jacket or a sweater or even raingear? Is it early or late in a round and how loose do you feel? Are you pumped up or tired? In other words, think about any factor that could influence your club selection. As you practice and play more, you will get better and better at determining how far you generally hit each club and, therefore, given the questions you have asked, you should be able to make the right club selection.

Remember one last thing when it comes to club selection: Most amateurs allow their egos to get in the way and they often select too little club. I once read an article by Sam Snead that contended that if you tracked how many times amateurs overshoot a green or their target compared with how many times they are short of the green or their target, you would find they are short many more times than long. A rule of thumb might be: When in doubt, use one more club—unless there is much more trouble (a lake, sand, woods, etc.) behind the target than in front of it.

Once you have completed your club selection, go behind the ball and focus your attention and energy on the target. Your task now is to hit with the club you have selected as well as you possibly can. It is at this time that you *should begin the first step of the teaching process—clearly defining what you would like to achieve* on this particular shot. This step is key for programming your mind. You see, our mind is a computer. Some people say it is the greatest computer ever made. But like any outstanding computer, its performance depends on the quality of the software being used. Who's in charge of your software? Who's in charge of programming your mind? You are! If you send your mind good information wrapped in positive thoughts, it will function well in your best interests. If you program your mind with bad information and negative thoughts, it will respond in kind.

How do you *program your mind?* As we suggested in the last chapter, there are *three ways* to clarify the task to be performed depending on your learning style: *verbally, visually and kinesthetically.* We translated those approaches into "tell," "show," and "experience." Auditory learners process information best through hearing and, therefore, function well with the "tell" approach. Visual learners, on the other hand, like to see what they are learning and, therefore, are attracted to the "show" approach. Finally, kinesthetic learners are people who are extraordinarily sensitive to touch and how things feel physically, and, therefore, respond to an "experience" or a "feel" approach.

The main purpose in clarifying the task is to give your mind direction. It's important to know how you learn best: by hearing information, seeing it or feeling/experiencing it. While an effective instructor will use all three learning styles in teaching you, most people have a favorite style. It is important to know your own best learning style, since the answer will impact how you should give your mind direction.

The S.E.A. (Sports Enhancement Associates) golf schools that Chuck Hogan runs emphasize an approach tailored to each individual's learning style. I've learned from Chuck that I am predominantly an *auditory* learner. Therefore, verbal commands are most effective in programming my mind. Jay Sigel, who has won every amateur title possible, is a *visual* learner. He needs to picture what he is going to do. Lynn Marriott, who is a fine golfer, is a *kinesthetic* learner. She has to feel what she is going to do.

Since Lynn Marriott is a kinesthetic learner, visualization techniques are not effective for her. In fact, when she concentrates on visual images, she usually hits a bad shot. She needs to feel connected to her target. What works for Lynn is to feel as if her ball is on a wavelength or vibration to the target, and that all she has to do is get the club head and the ball to meet on that wavelength or vibration.

As a visual learner, Jay Sigel has to see the results of his shot. When he is playing in a tournament, he makes sure he is familiar with the course so that he knows how to play a hole before he actually plays it. If it calls for a left-to-right shot or a right-to-left shot, he has to picture that shot when programming his mind.

As an auditory learner, I literally talk my way to the target. I verbally program my mind. I find I do best when I imitate Bill Murray in the movie *Caddyshack:* "Here we are at Augusta. He's about 165 yards from the hole. Slight wind in his face, a 5-iron in his hand. The pin is tucked to the right behind a huge trap." The words I say are not as important as their sound and the rhythm I get from them. People who play with me laugh about my chatter. I don't do it to bother anyone. It just makes my brain and body work better. No matter how you do it, the intent of clarifying the task to be performed is to program your mind to connect your shot with the target.

Neither Jay nor Lynn thinks about his/her swing during the pre-shot routine. Most good golfers think "swing thoughts" are for the practice tee when they are working on something specific. On the course, the focus of their pre-shot routine is completely on the target, not on the swing.

Since my golf game is not as developed as either Lynn's or Jay's, I *still* find it helpful to have some swing thoughts during my pre-shot routine. You may too. As a result, when I take a practice swing behind the ball, I might say to myself, "Get good upper body rotation on this shot and then, on the forward swing, move up and out toward the target." You will have your own key swing thoughts. All of us have different aspects of our swing we are trying to improve.

After you identify your task clearly, before you head up to the ball, you might want to program your mind for success. I first learned from Tony Robbins, author of the best-selling *Unlimited Power* and *Awaken the Giant Within*, and then relearned from Chuck Hogan, that there are three keys to programming your mind for success. The *first* is *positive thinking.* If you have played a fair amount of golf, think back to a time when you hit a great shot. When Jay Sigel has an important shot to hit, he just says to himself, "You've done it before and you can do it this time."

If you have not had any real success experiences with the shot you are about to take, imagine how you felt when you were doing something else well. Sometimes I put myself in the mind-set I had playing basketball when I was younger and I was hot. Every shot I took went in. I was in the zone: what we called "unconscious." I wanted the ball because I knew I could make the shot. I had a lot of energy.

Second, positive thinking has to be combined with appropriate positive physiology or *body language*. Positive thinking says to your mind, "I am confident. I can do this." Some people think positive thinking is enough to guarantee success. It's not! If you say, "I love sand shots," but as you approach the trap your head is down and your shoulders are drooping, you will be sending a mixed message to your mind. What will your mind believe? Your body language? Why? Because people's behavior means more than their words.

When working with clinically depressed people, Tony Robbins has found that one of the most helpful ways to get them out of a depression is to have them walk around saying, "I am happy and I feel great," with their shoulders back, their heads high, and big grins on their faces. With those verbal messages and that body language, it is much more difficult for them to be depressed.

So remember: It is not only important to think positively but to behave and act positively. So many golfers head up to the ball to hit a shot with low energy. They look as if they are defeated before they start.

Whatever you do before you hit a shot, make sure it is consistent with your personality. I'm an extrovert. When I head toward the ball I have a lot of energy. If I'm playing by myself I might even clap my hands and yell, "Let's go," like a football team does when it breaks huddle and heads to the line of scrimmage. That works for me but what will work for you? You need to get in touch with how you feel and how you behave when you are doing something well. Don't let your actions shortcut your positive thinking.

The *third* and final key to programming your mind positively is your *routine*. Peak performers seem to use the same routine every time they do something. In basketball good foul shooters bounce the ball the same number of times every time. Good putters approach the ball the same way every time. We all have to work out a winning routine. If you approach the ball differently every time, you send a confused message to your mind.

Jay Sigel feels that the pre-shot routine is very important for consistent shot production. He finds that he tends to hit shots best when he approaches the ball from the side. While he is walking, he continues to visualize the kind of shot he wants to hit. After Jay gets set, he bangs the club head on the ground, takes a couple of "waggles," and starts his swing.

Lynn Marriott also approaches the ball from the side, but she does not do it at a right angle. She walks toward the ball open to the target. She does that because she favors her right side and feels more comfortable and committed to the target from that side. When she gets to the ball, she sets the club head once and very decisively behind the ball; this connects her with where she is going—the target. Then she puts her club on "the conveyor belt to the target" and begins her swing. Whatever you do, remember:

*

*Positive thinking
combined
with
congruent body language
and
a clear routine
will program
your mind
for
success*

*

I had a dramatic example of improvement using these three keys to success. I had played nine holes just before a trip to Chicago and I had shot the worst nine-hole round I can remember—a 54. I was really discouraged about my game. On the way back from Chicago I met Tony Robbins on the plane. I told him about my awful round, and he said, "It sounds like you weren't programmed for success." With that he taught me the power of positive thinking, congruent body language, and a clear routine. The next day I rushed to the course and played the same nine holes I did before my trip—and shot a 39. It works!

Swing Routine

At this point you have completed your pre-shot routine and are ready to execute—that is, to hit the shot. As you head to the ball, you cross what Chuck Hogan calls "the decision line." Now you move from "thinking" to "doing." Most experienced golfers and teachers agree that too much focus on swing thoughts before you hit the ball may immobilize you. Tim Gallwey, who wrote *The Inner Game of Tennis* and then followed it with *The Inner Game of Golf,* explains it well. He argues that achievement is a result of skill minus interference. What is interference? All the little "self-talk" you are filling your head with at the point when you want just to be applying your skills constitutes interference.

Once when Tim and I were on a program together at an executive retreat, I saw him do a mind-blowing exercise. He asked if there was anyone there who could not catch a ball. A woman raised her hand and said, "For some reason I've never been able to catch a ball."

Tim had a very soft Nerf ball and asked if she'd be willing to help him. The woman agreed. Tim said, "What I'm going to do is throw this soft ball to you underhand. See if you can catch it." Tim lobbed the ball toward the woman four or five times. What do you think he proved? She couldn't catch a ball. Every time he threw it toward her, she would fumble it.

Tim said, "OK. I'm going to throw this ball toward you again. This time, don't think about trying to catch the ball. What I want you to do is watch the ball as it comes toward you and count how many times the ball fully rotates from when it leaves my hand to when it gets to you." The result was incredible! As Tim threw the ball toward the woman, she reached up and caught the ball and shouted, "Three." Then, "That time it was four." And then, "I think that was three again," as she caught the ball every time. Finally realizing what was happening, she said, "I can't believe it. I'm catching the ball."

How did she suddenly learn how to catch the ball? She wasn't concentrating on catching it; her mind was focused on something else. Tim realized this phenomenon when he began teaching people to play tennis. One of the reasons he found that players weren't hitting the ball well was that they were paralyzed by swing mechanics—"Get low, keep your right elbow close to your body," etc. Students had much better luck hitting the tennis ball when Tim had them say to themselves "back-hit" as the ball came toward them. With players saying "back-hit" every time they approached the ball, tennis began to become much easier for them. Why? Because their minds were filled with "back-hit," not with swing mechanics.

When Tim transferred his inner game to golf, he added an additional word. As they were swinging the club, he asked golfers to say to themselves "back-hit-finish." With the addition of the third word, he emphasized the importance of the follow-through. I find that saying these three words to myself during my golf swing increases significantly the number of good shots I hit. And that's not only true for my full swing, but also pitching, chipping, sand play, and putting. This gets me into almost a meditative state. If you haven't meditated yourself, you've undoubtedly heard people talk about meditation. During meditation the intention is to quiet your mind. If your mind is very active in the beginning of meditation, it is often suggested that you use some mantra like "one, one, one" or a chant to fill your mind and keep thoughts away. Saying "back-hit-finish" will do that very thing for you during your golf swing. You programmed your mind with swing thoughts behind the ball. As you actually swing the club, you must trust that those swing thoughts are still in place. Reprogramming your mind during your swing will only confuse things.

I learned another technique to keep my mind clear of new thoughts when swinging from Tom Crum, author of *The Magic of Conflict*. Tom is also an expert in *aikido*, an Eastern form of self-defense. In *aikido*, if someone goes to punch you, they tell you not to try to block the punch. When you try to block a punch, you are using resistance—your power and strength against the other person's power and strength. *That* sets up a win-lose confrontation.

In *aikido*, they step aside with an accepting and pivoting movement, using the attacker's energy to throw him or to apply a neutralizing technique. The key for all this, as Tom teaches it, is to learn how to be centered, with both mind and body relaxed and alert. It is in this state of heightened awareness and connectedness that thinking about mechanics ceases and the flow, or zone, begins.

According to Tom, you can let go of some of those interfering technical thoughts on the course by focusing on simple physiological responses like breathing. All great athletic movements are done fluidly without tension. If the breathing is full and continuous, so is the body's state of movement and relaxation. If the breath is held or shallow, the body's movements will be correspondingly rigid and discontinuous. Smooth and powerful breathing can be correlated with smooth tempo and consistent long shot making.

Applying this principle to golf, Tom suggests that you try "breathing in" on your backswing and "breathing out" on your forward swing, and to visualize the breath running all the way through to the clubhead and out.

Now, I realize there are a lot of jokes about how it is possible to mess up someone's game during a match by asking, "Do you breathe in or breathe out on your backswing?" What Tom is saying about breathing in on your backswing and breathing out on your forward swing is no joke. If you've ever seen Jimmy Connors serve a tennis ball and heard him almost shout out when he hits the ball, you've seen what Tom is talking about. Good tennis players breathe in as they toss the ball up on their serve; then breathe out as they hit the ball. This gives them increased power; weight lifters do the same thing when they exert themselves. In golf, breathing will not only give you additional power, but concentrating on breathing in and then breathing out will keep you from thinking about swing mechanics when you swing.

I had a wonderful success experience using *aikido* breathing techniques several years ago, when I had an opportunity to play Cypress Point on the Monterey Peninsula—one of the greatest courses in the world. I was playing with Bill Borland, the president of the club at the time. When we got to the famous sixteenth hole—a 235-yard carry across the ocean—Bill suggested that we take the short way over the water and play the hole as a par 4.

I said, "No way! I didn't come here to play it safe. I'm going to show you how to hit it over the water using *aikido* breathing." Everyone in my foursome laughed and said, "We'll have to see this." Well, I teed the ball up and then stood behind it. I told myself, "I want a good shoulder turn and then a strong finish through the ball." Then I took a practice swing that felt good, and as I swung through the ball I could hear a great explosion and I visualized the ball sailing over the water, landing on the green, and rolling toward the hole. Then I got myself energized, squeezed my fist, and headed toward the ball with confidence.

As I headed toward the ball, I used my Caddyshack chatter to get into a good frame of mind. Then, once settled over the ball, I began to breathe in while I started my backswing. As I got to the top of my swing and began my forward swing, I started to breathe out with a loud crescendo as I hit the ball and followed through. The ball exploded off the tee. Bill shouted, "I can't believe it!" as the ball sailed across the ocean, landed three feet on the other side, and then bounced up on the green and rolled to within about two feet of the cup. I had a tap-in birdie on what is considered the toughest par 3 in the world. (There have been only a few holes in one on this hole in the history of the club.) For me to hit a drive that carries in the air over 230 yards was incredible. I had been telling Bill Borland all about positive thinking and *aikido* throughout the round; with that shot alone, I might have made him a believer.

The key point I want to make here is that when you get over the ball, don't think swing mechanics. Do something to keep your mind busy, like saying a silent mantra such as "one, one, one," or "back-hit-finish," or "breathe in–breathe out." Then just hit the ball. You programmed your mind with swing thoughts behind the ball, now it's time for Nike golf—just do it!

Post-shot Routine

Now you're ready for the final steps: *Observation* and *Praise Progress* and/or *Redirect*. After you hit your shot, you observe the results. The first thing you want to look for is anything praiseworthy in the shot. Behind the ball you set your goal for the shot. After you hit the shot, you move to the second secret of the One Minute Manager: One Minute Praising. In the previous chapter we talked about your instructor praising any progress you make. Now that you are a self-managed player, the responsibility falls to you. When is the last time you caught yourself doing something right on the golf course? Unless you're unusual, you hardly ever praise yourself on the golf course. Most of the time you're catching yourself doing things wrong. Remember:

*

*The
key
to
improving
your golf
is
to
catch yourself
doing things
right*

*

There are three parts to an effective praising. First, praise yourself *immediately*—don't save it up until the end of the round. Second, *be specific*—what did you like: the direction, the length, the results, or some part of the swing? Just saying to yourself, "Good shot" is not helpful enough. If you want to repeat something, you have to let your mind know what you liked. And third, with an effective praising, you *express how you feel* about the shot—excited, happy, encouraged, whatever you are feeling.

Praising is all about self-talk, and the self-talk of most golfers is completely negative. Most golfers beat themselves up around the golf course. It's hard for some people to be their own best friend and pat themselves on the back. I played with a fellow once who started to yell at himself, "You idiot! How could you be so stupid?" almost before he even hit the ball. No matter what happened, it was never good enough. I recommended that he quit the game. He didn't think I was serious, but I was. He found nothing he did was praiseworthy.

A praising is particularly powerful when you are just learning or relearning a particular shot, because you can catch yourself doing things approximately right, not exactly right. Bob Toski, in our article "The One Minute Golfer," tells the One Minute Manager a wonderful story about someone who didn't believe in approximately right:

> *The other day I was giving a lesson to a fairly decent player, not an average player. He hit a shot a little off line. No sooner had he hit the shot, than he said, "I missed it."*
>
> *His negative attitude really got to me. He had been like that throughout the lesson. So I said, "Wait a minute! What do you mean you missed it?"*

I grabbed his club from him and said, "I'll show you a miss." I put a ball down and fanned it.

"That's a miss," I said. "You hit that ball and you don't know how good you actually hit it. I'm going to show you some bad shots." I lined up several balls and hit some awful shots. Then I shouted, "Did your ball do that?"

"No," he said meekly, kind of taken aback by my seeming anger.

"Well then," I countered, "you are evidently a perfectionist trying to seek perfection. I didn't ask you to hit a perfect shot. Have I ever asked you during this lesson to hit a perfect shot?"

"No," he said.

"I have asked you to try and hit the ball a certain way and get it moving forward and outward and you are doing that. . . ."

"I give it to people straight because I care and want them to improve," said Toski. "If this guy I was teaching waited until he hit a shot exactly right before he patted himself on the back, he might wait forever."

You have to remember that hitting great shots is a result of hitting a whole bunch of approximately right shots. If you hit a real "worm burner" that races along the ground but is straight, praise yourself for the straightness.

For example, one day when I was playing I really belted a 5-wood, but it went over the top of a house and out-of-bounds. I shouted out, "Wow! Did I hit that shot? I really made great contact." The fellow I was playing with said, "Blanchard, you're something. You hit a ball out-of-bounds. It cost you a two-stroke penalty. And you're patting yourself on the back."

I said, "I know, but I did make good contact so I at least wanted to praise that much. Now the next shot I want to make sure I get a good shoulder turn and then finish my swing. On that shot I didn't finish my swing."

You see, after you praise any progress, you need to redirect your efforts so that you can perform even better on the next shot. Watch the pros. When they make a mistake—they miss a putt or don't hit a shot right—what do they do? They take a practice swing right then. That's their way of redirecting themselves so they won't make the same mistake the next time.

Do you always need to redirect yourself? No. If you hit a great shot, then pat yourself on the back and do an "Arnold Palmer": Hitch your pants up and charge down the fairway.

Do good players praise themselves? Sure! Remember Jay Sigel's inner smile? Lynn Marriott accentuates a good shot with a "hmmmmmm!" She says it is her "after shot mantra." She also brings her club back around to her address position after she has swung it. This is kind of a physical, kinesthetic praising.

What if you hit a shot with no redeeming qualities? As we suggested earlier, don't give a bad shot much emotion. If, however, you are a person who just can't hold back feelings, giving yourself a One Minute Reprimand might be helpful. But remember, a reprimand is only appropriate if you have had some success with that shot in the past. If you are just learning it, though, redirection is more appropriate than a reprimand. A good distinction here is whether the poor result is a problem of "can't do" (ability) or "won't do" (attitude). If it's an ability problem—you are still learning—redirection is best. If, however, it is an attitude problem, then a reprimand might be warranted.

Remember, the rules of a reprimand are somewhat similar to the One Minute Praising with one addition: the reaffirmation. But first, you must deliver the reprimand *immediately*—right after the bad shot. Second, be *specific*. Don't just say, "That was a lousy shot." What was specifically bad about it? The results, of course, but what caused the bad results? For example, you didn't get a good turn, you started your forward swing with your right side, or you essentially stopped your swing at the ball. If you're not sure, ask one of your playing partners. The more specific you are about a bad shot, the better chance you'll have of correcting it in the future.

Third, after identifying what you did wrong, a good reprimand permits you to *express your feelings* about a bad shot. "That really ticks me off. It drives me crazy." Most people don't have any trouble with that part of the reprimand on the golf course. Just a look at their face tells you if they are disgusted, angry, disappointed, or what. It's the fourth part of the reprimand they have a problem with—the *reaffirmation*.

After they express their feelings about a bad shot, most golfers beat themselves up. They call themselves every name in the book, "You idiot," "stupid," and the like. When you do that, you forget one of the cardinal rules of One Minute Management:

*

I'm OK
it's just
my behavior
that's
a
problem
sometimes

*

When you reaffirm, you essentially tell yourself that you are "better than that." You need to tell yourself how unlike you this specific behavior is: "The reason I am upset is that I am a better golfer than that shot indicates."

The reaffirmation at the end of the reprimand is probably the most important part, because it clearly separates out your behavior—the bad shot—from your self-worth. So many golfers forget that. They mistreat themselves on the course. If you do that, it's hard to prepare for the next shot without still thinking about the last one. So, always end a reprimand with positive energy to get yourself ready to perform better the next time. If you really get down on yourself, things will go from bad to worse.

What I hope you can see now is *how you will behave if you are a self-managed player.* You will be able to *clarify by yourself the task to be accomplished,* then *do it, observe your results,* and finally, *praise any progress and/or redirect.* What this process does is keep you on track by helping you constantly monitor your performance in relation to your intended goals.

Stay in the Present

Let me overlay one final Zen concept on these teaching-learning steps. It has to do with time orientation. Spencer Johnson who co-authored *The One Minute Manager* talks about it in his brilliant parable *The Precious Present.* Let me see if I can share how it applies to golf.

There are three time orientations—past, present, and future. When you're setting your goals behind the ball, what time orientation are you in? You are planning the future by programming your mind in terms of what you are hoping to do. When you are over the ball getting ready to hit your shot, what time orientation should you be in? You should be in the present. And, finally, after you hit the ball, what time orientation should prevail? You should be analyzing the past and then, when appropriate, planning the future through redirection.

It is important not to mix up these time orientations when you are playing golf. It is particularly dangerous to contaminate the present with past negative feelings or future aspirations. And yet this happens all the time on the golf course. I have seen players, for example, hit a putt on the first hole and have it stop on the lip because the greenskeeper did not cut the cup right. Rather than learning from that experience and hitting their putts on future holes firmer around the cup, they let this bad experience ruin their entire round. Even on the fifteenth hole, rather than focusing on the putt at hand, they are still complaining about the greenskeeper and the poorly cut cups. What do you think is the result? Another poor putt.

I've seen people do the same with future orientation. How many times have you been playing an all-time-best career round with three holes left to play, when suddenly, your game falls apart. Although you only need to bogey these last three holes to record your best round ever, you find yourself double-bogeying the next two holes and your career round is a thing of the past. Why does that happen? Rather than staying in the present and focusing on each shot one at a time, you are already seeing yourself in the clubhouse bragging to your buddies and calling old partners to tell them the good news.

In the 1986 Masters, Jack Nicklaus was a beautiful example of someone catching himself from going to the future too early. On the eighteenth hole, in the middle of his dramatic charge for a sixth Masters championship, Jack's second shot hit the slope in the middle of the green and rolled back down away from the cup. This left him with about a fifty-foot putt uphill for a birdie. As Jack headed for the green, the gallery went wild and gave him one of the most thunderous ovations ever. Jack reported later that his eyes began to fill with tears. He was so touched by the crowd and this historic scene at Augusta: Winning a sixth championship would be the ultimate triumph. "I suddenly caught myself," Jack reported later. Then, chastising himself, he said, "Jack, there is more golf to play." Without that redirection Jack might have lost his present-time focus and three-putted the tournament away.

The important thing for you to remember is that when you are over the ball, you should forget what happened in the past and not worry or think about the future. The only shot you have is the one right now. After you hit the shot, you analyze it and plan for the future and then move on to the next shot. The best time orientation you can have over a golf shot is the precious present. Just hit it!

CHAPTER 6

Commitment: What Can You Do to Follow Through on Your Good Intentions?

Golf is a game where guts, stick-to-itiveness . . . and blind devotion will always net you absolutely nothing but an ulcer.
—Tommy Bolt
PGA Hall of Fame

Thisbook is about playing the great game of golf and making every *minute* count. My hope was to help you enjoy golf more. Giving you an ulcer, as Tommy Bolt suggests you'll get from golf, was not my intention. And I don't think it should be yours. Golf is a *game* and should be played for enjoyment. And yet, how can you follow through on your good intentions and achieve the results you desire? Let's review the journey we have taken in this book and see if we can find some answers.

In Part One, GOLF AND YOU, we talked in Chapter 1 about why you play golf. This involved thinking about purpose. Remember, purpose is your intention—something toward which you are always striving. It is ongoing. It is not something you can accomplish and then stop worrying about. It is your reason for playing. When you are clear about your purpose, you can keep your ego under control; patience and persistence will become your friends; and you will be able to keep your golf game in perspective.

What is (are) your purpose(s)? Why do you play golf? These are questions you need to answer for yourself and then observe and monitor your behavior to see how well you are doing in relation to your purpose(s). Sometimes people say they play golf for one reason and then their behavior does not follow.

Take a minute to list as many reasons as possible why you think you play golf. Think only about big-picture things that do not depend on how you score, things like having fun, enjoying people, appreciating the beauty around you, competing against yourself or others, etc.

—————————————— • ——————————————

—————————————— • ——————————————

—————————————— • ——————————————

—————————————— • ——————————————

—————————————— • ——————————————

Prioritize your list. Select the three reasons that are most compelling for you. Rank them in importance from 1 to 3.

My Number One purpose for playing golf is:

—————————————————————————————

—————————————————————————————

My Number Two purpose for playing golf is:

_____

_____

My Number Three purpose for playing golf is:

_____

_____

Focus on the purpose that you listed as Number One. Take one minute to answer the question: How will you know when that purpose is being fulfilled when you play golf? Be specific!

_____

_____

_____

_____

What do you need to think, feel, or do when you play golf to fulfill this purpose?

_____

_____

_____

_____

Focus on the purpose that you listed as Number Two. Take one minute to answer the question: How will you know when that purpose is being fulfilled when you play golf? Be specific!

_____

_____

_____

What do you need to think, feel, or do when you play golf to fulfill this purpose?

_____

_____

Focus on the purpose that you listed as Number Three. Take one minute to answer the question: How will you know when that purpose is being fulfilled when you play golf. Be specific!

_____

_____

_____

What do you need to think, feel, or do when you play golf to fulfill this purpose?

_____

_____

_____

In Chapter 2 we moved to goal setting and focused on what you want to accomplish with your golf game. A goal is not a purpose. A goal is tangible. It is something you can accomplish: reducing your handicap, winning your flight at your club, or shooting a certain score. Remember: *All good performance starts with clear goals.*

Take a minute to list those things that you would like to accomplish that will make you feel good about your golf game.

_____ • _____

_____ • _____

_____ • _____

_____ • _____

_____ • _____

Prioritize your list. Select the three most engaging goals from your list. Rank them in importance from 1 to 3.

My Number One goal is:

_____

_____

My Number Two goal is:

_____

_____

My Number Three goal is:

_____

_____

Focus on the goal that you listed as Number One. Take one minute to answer the question: How will you know when you have achieved this goal? Be specific!

_____

_____

_____

What knowledge or skill do you need to accomplish that goal?

_____

_____

_____

_____

What action can you take, on a daily basis, to make this goal a reality?

_____

_____

_____

_____

Focus on the goal that you listed as Number Two. Take one minute to answer the question: How will you know when you have achieved this goal?

_____

_____

_____

_____

What knowledge or skill do you need to accomplish that goal?

_____

_____

_____

_____

What action can you take, on a daily basis, to make this goal a reality?

_____

_____

_____

_____

Focus on the goal you listed as Number Three. Take one minute to answer the question: How will you know when you have achieved this goal?

_____

_____

_____

_____

What knowledge or skill do you need to accomplish that goal?

_____

_____

_____

_____

What action can you take, on a daily basis, to make this goal a reality?

_____

_____

_____

_____

Look a second time at all of the actions that you can take on a daily basis to achieve your goals. Realistically trim that list by working SMART.

Eliminate any action that is not *S*pecific
Eliminate any action that is not *M*otivational
Eliminate any action that is not *A*ttainable
Eliminate any action that is not *R*elevant
Eliminate any action that is not *T*rackable

Below list actions which, if done on a daily basis, would help you to accomplish your goals. These tasks could include practice ideas, exercise routines, or self-management techniques.

I commit to accomplishing the following tasks on a daily basis to enjoy golf more and achieve the results I desire:

_____

_____

_____

_____

_____

_____

_____

Signature

_____

Date

In Part Two, GETTING BETTER AT GOLF, we discussed in Chapter 3 why it is difficult to improve or change. As I think about change, I am struck again and again by the power of one concept. Now that you have set a course of action for yourself, remember that the key to enjoying golf more and achieving the results you desire is:

*

Catch yourself doing things right

*

On a daily basis, every time that you accomplish your tasks for the day, stop for a moment to savor the accomplishment. Then anchor that emotion with an inward smile.

In this way you will direct and support yourself toward the habits you wish to acquire.

On days when you don't accomplish your tasks, give yourself a One Minute Reprimand, without emotion, and then redirect yourself toward the behavior you desire.

Relapse is normal. Get yourself back on track as soon as possible. Remember: It does not matter how slow you go as long as you do not stop.

Chapter 4 encouraged you to become your own coach. Whom do you know who could be your mentor and help you manage your own journey to better golf?

Why did you choose that person?

When will you contact that person?

How will you ensure that your mentor will help you become a self-managed player?

If you want to see a good example of a mentor, rent the movie *The Karate Kid*. In that film, Miyagi, played by Pat Morita, is able to teach a teenager by the name of Daniel to become a karate champion by shifting his leadership style from directing to coaching to supporting and delegating. He moves Daniel from being a dependent learner to a self-managed performer. Find a mentor! A friend, a professional golf instructor, a golf school. Start your journey soon.

In Part Three, MAINTAINING YOUR PROGRESS, you learned in Chapter 5 what to do on the course if you were your own coach. You learned to (1) *see, hear,* or *feel* what your correct behavior should be; (2) *execute* that behavior; (3) *observe* that behavior; and finally, (4) *praise progress and/or redirect* your efforts. If you learn to go through those four steps religiously as part of preparing, hitting, and analyzing every shot, I guarantee that you will play better golf and enjoy it more. The choice is yours! That's where commitment and behaving on your good intentions come into play.

A lot of people who have read various drafts of this book have said, "Ken, this is fabulous! I really want to use this philosophy to become my own coach and play better golf." My typical response is, "I'm not concerned about your commitment. I'm concerned about your commitment to your commitment." Remember, diets work fine; people don't. They break their commitments. How many golf books do you need to make a difference in your golf game? Only the one that you stick to; we hope that this book is going to be the one. After you finish reading it, share it with your family, your friends, your golf pro, even your playing partners—anyone who would like to see you improve your game. Ask them to help you stick to your commitment.

A friend of mine, Art Turock, who wrote *Getting Physical,* taught me the difference between commitment and interest. People who are interested in improving their golf game will always have an excuse for why they can't practice or play. On the other hand, committed people don't know about excuses; they just know about results. If they say they are going to practice, they do. If they say they are going to play, they do. I know a lot of people who are interested in being good golfers but are not committed to it. They're like an interested exerciser who wakes up in the morning and says, "It's raining. I think I'll exercise tomorrow." A committed exerciser would say, "It's raining. I'd better put on my rain gear."

Recall why you play golf and what you want to accomplish. Do you want to be a champion or just enjoy playing more, or do you want something in between? How good a golfer do you want to be? How much are you going to practice? How important is golf to you? What is your commitment?

Some people come to the Golf University who are golf school "goers," and they think their main task is to evaluate our program. Is it as good as the Golf Digest School? Or how does it compare to the John Jacobs schools? We had one man who had gone to six different schools but showed no significant improvement. He was a classic golf school "goer."

What we want is a golf "doer." Someone who is going to take what he or she has learned and do something with it. The difference between a "goer" and a "doer" is best described by the story of the man who, climbing a mountain, trips and falls over the side. Luckily he is able to grab a branch and hold on for dear life. He looks down and 1,500 feet below is a rockbed valley. He looks up and it's about 20 feet from where he fell. He starts to yell, "Help! Help! Is there anybody up there?"

A big, booming voice answers him: "Yes. I am here. I will help you if you believe in me." How many of you believe in the things I've taught you in this book? I bet a lot of you.

The guy yells, "I believe. I believe."

Then the voice says (just as I do), "If you believe in me, let go of the branch and I will save you." Of course, the guy let go of the branch and was saved. What is the branch? All the excuses; all the reasons why you can't follow up on what you've learned and what you know you should be doing.

(The best description of the branch was told to me by a friend one day after he had eaten lunch at a manufacturing plant. At the next table a group of workers sat down. One man opened his lunch box and started to yell, "Bologna sandwich again! This is the fourth straight day I've had a bologna sandwich and I hate bologna."

"Relax! Relax!" said one of his friends. "Why don't you ask your wife to make a different sandwich?"

"My wife, hell!" said the worker. "I made the sandwiches myself." So the branch is all of our bologna.)

Golf "doers" would drop the branch without hesitation. They are ready to let go of the past and do what it takes to improve.

Golf "goers," on the other hand, would look down and then up again and yell, "Is there anybody else up there?" The golf "goer" is looking for the next golf school, the next lesson, the next book. He or she doesn't understand. It's not the next golf school or lesson or book that makes the difference. It's your commitment to following through on your commitment. It's doing what you said you were going to do. This can be absolutely the best golf book you've ever read if you make and keep your agreement to apply and use what you've learned from it. Go for it!

AFTERWORD
by Chuck Hogan

Is this a golf instruction book? Or is it a statement of golfing philosophy? I wonder if it is a guide to discovery and self-management on the golf course. The answer is, it is. *Playing the Great Game of Golf* is a book about all of those things and many more.

Some readers may not find this to be a book of golf instruction. This book does not insist that you do this or that in a certain fashion. More important, it does not say that if you do not follow the prescribed lessons, you will fail. Nowhere are there side-by-side pictures labeled "correct" and "incorrect." Nowhere does the book say "Do it MY way." How refreshing.

Each of us who reads this book is left with a new and broadened perspective of what golf is about. Or maybe it gives a perspective on what each of us is like as we learn and play golf. The perspective is also on what we learn about ourselves as we participate in the game. Now, some hard-core veteran golfers shun the idea that there is a philosophical side to golf. Nevertheless, even they will admit that golf forces introspection—to the marrow.

This book is REfreshing. It is not fresh. It is largely a return to the essence of the game the way golfers learned and played the game from Day One until thirty years (or so) ago. Golf was virtually never taught until the last three decades. Golf was always learned. There were very few formal instructors. By today's standards, there was no golfing industry to speak of. Golf was still a game, and people learned it by PLAYING the game. And PLAY they did. Underneath the play, the learning went on and on and on. This book is a REiteration of the nature of the game as it existed for eons. It is a healthy thing to return golf as a game.

On the other hand, this book does not ignore the technical and strategic considerations that have become pervasive in the last three decades. Golfers have been overwhelmed with analysis, particularly in the last fifteen years. Golf instruction has simply mirrored our culture's pursuit of technical saturation. Thankfully, these pages reduce crippling technical and intellectual analysis by reframing "how to's" into a flow of events that allows the reader/golfer to go through a process leading to the self-ownership of the learned. Ah, now here is the essence of the game. What a concept!

To play and discover and create and get lost and return to home base and to be safe and at ease with oneself. Then to do it all again and again and again, always open to new and wonderful experiences and opportunities to discover anew. A game of "re-creation."

Re-creation is available only from home base; the place where the player is the owner of the creation.

Thank goodness that there is a way to make every minute count. Thank goodness there is, again, a reference for that long lost anchor: It is not whether you win or lose, it is how you PLAY the GAME. Thanks, Ken.

—Chuck Hogan

PART FOUR

APPENDIX

NOTES/REFERENCES

Introduction

Notes

1. Kenneth Blanchard and Spencer Johnson, *The One Minute Manager* (New York: William Morrow and Company, Inc., 1982), p. 67.

References

Blanchard, Kenneth, and Bob Toski. "The One Minute Golfer." *Golf Digest,* June 1985.
———, D. W. Edington, and Marjorie Blanchard. *The One Minute Manager Gets Fit.* New York: William Morrow and Company, Inc., 1986.
———, and Norman Vincent Peale. *The Power of Ethical Management.* New York: William Morrow and Company, Inc., 1988.
Hogan, Chuck. *Five Days to Golfing Excellence.* Sedona, Ariz.: T & C Publishing, 1986.
Peale, Norman Vincent. *The Power of Positive Thinking.* Englewood Cliffs, N.J.: Prentice-Hall, 1952.

PART ONE: GOLF AND YOU
Chapter 1: Purpose: Why Do You Play Golf?

Notes

1. Kenneth Blanchard and Norman Vincent Peale, *The Power of Ethical Management* (New York: William Morrow and Company, Inc., 1988), pp. 42–80.
2. Michael Murphy, *Golf in the Kingdom* (New York: Penguin Books/Arkana, 1992), p. 78.
3. Ibid.

4. Gary Player, quoted in "1986 MASTERS TOUR-NAMENT," video (Augusta, Ga.: Augusta National Golf Club, 1986).

5. Roy Benjamin, "In Defense of the Multi-hued, Peaked Capped Hacker," Gannett Westchester Newspapers, May 1986, White Plains, N.Y.

6. Murphy, p. 137.

7. Benjamin, "In Defense . . ."

References

Kushner, Harold S. *When All You've Ever Wanted Isn't Enough*. Boston, Mass.: G. K. Hall, 1987.

———. *When Bad Things Happen to Good People*. Boston, Mass.: G. K. Hall, 1982.

PART ONE: GOLF AND YOU
Chapter 2: Goal Setting: What Do You Want to Accomplish?

Notes

1. I first learned the SMART acronym from colleague and friend Ken Haff. A suggested change in "M" from "Measurable" to "Motivational" was made by Laurence Hawkins and Susan Fowler-Woodring in their work on "Situational Self-Leadership," a Blanchard Training and Development product.

2. David C. McClelland, J. W. Atkinson, R. A. Clark, and E. L. Lowell, *The Achievement Motive* (New York: Appleton-Century Crofts, 1953), and McClelland, *The Achieving Society* (Princeton, N.J.: D. Van Nostrand, 1961).

3. Charles A. Garfield and Hal Z. Bennett, *Peak Performance: Mental Training Techniques of the World's Greatest Athletes* (New York: J. P. Tarcher, 1984).

4. D. Swing Meyer, *The Method: A Golf Success Strategy* (Columbia, S.C.: Acorn Sports, 1981), p. 3.

5. Ibid., p. 8.

6. Kenneth Blanchard and Norman Vincent Peale, *The Power of Ethical Management* (New York: William Morrow and Company, Inc., 1988), p. 18–27.

References

Blanchard, Kenneth, Donald Carew, and Eunice-Parisi Carew. *The One Minute Manager Builds High Performing Teams*. New York: William Morrow and Company, Inc., 1991.

The Official Rules of Golf (instructional video), explained by Tom Watson and Peter Alliss. Westport, Conn.: Caravatt Communications, Inc.

PART TWO: GETTING BETTER AT GOLF
Chapter 3: Change: Why Is It Difficult to Learn New Habits?

Notes

1. Paul Hersey and Kenneth H. Blanchard, *Management of Organizational Behavior*, 5th ed. (Englewood Cliffs, N.J.: Prentice-Hall, 1988), pp. 3–4.

References

Blanchard, Kenneth, and Bob Toski. "The One Minute Golfer." *Golf Digest*, June 1985.

———, and Spencer Johnson. *The One Minute Manager*. New York: William Morrow and Company, Inc., 1982.

PART TWO: GETTING BETTER AT GOLF
Chapter 4: Instruction: How to Become Your Own Coach

Notes

1. Kenneth Blanchard and Spencer Johnson, *The One Minute Manager* (New York: William Morrow and Company, Inc., 1982).
2. Situational Leadership was first developed by Paul Hersey and Kenneth Blanchard at the Center for Leadership Studies. It was initially published by Hersey and Blanchard as "Life Cycle Theory of Leadership," in *Training and Development Journal,* May 1969; then it was discussed extensively in *Management of Organizational Behavior,* published by Prentice-Hall and now in its fifth edition. In the last decade, Blanchard and his colleagues at Blanchard Training and Development, Inc., have modified the original Situational Leadership model based on research and extensive feedback from managers. Their current approach to Situational Leadership, called SLII®, is described in Kenneth Blanchard, Patricia Zigarmi, and Drea Zigarmi, *Leadership and the One Minute Manager* (New York: William Morrow and Company, Inc., 1985). It is this version of Situational Leadership® that is used in this chapter.

PART THREE: MAINTAINING YOUR PROGRESS
Chapter 5: Application: How Do You Use What You've Learned?

References

Blanchard, Kenneth, and Bob Toski. "The One Minute Golfer." *Golf Digest,* June 1985.
———, and Spencer Johnson. *The One Minute Manager.* New York: William Morrow and Company, Inc., 1982.
Crum, Thomas F. *The Magic of Conflict.* New York: Simon & Schuster, 1987.

Egosque, Peter, with Roger Gittines. *The Egosque Method: Health Through Motion.* New York: Harper Collins, 1992.

Gallwey, Timothy W. *The Inner Game of Golf.* New York: Random House, 1981.

———. *The Inner Game of Tennis.* New York: Random House, 1974.

Hogan, Chuck, and David Witt. *Playing the Game: A Handbook for Golfers,* unpublished.

Jobe, Frank W., and Diane R. Moynes. *Thirty Exercises for Better Golf.* Inglewood, Calif.: Champion Press, 1989.

Johnson, Spencer. *The Precious Present.* New York: Doubleday, 1984.

Robbins, Anthony. *Awaken the Giant Within.* New York: Summit Books, 1991.

———. *Unlimited Power.* New York: Simon & Schuster, 1986.

PART THREE: MAINTAINING YOUR PROGRESS
Chapter 6: Commitment: What Can You Do to Follow Through on Your Good Intentions?

References

Turock, Art. *Getting Physical.* New York: Doubleday, 1988.

PRAISINGS

*P*laying the Great Game of Golf is the first book I have written by myself. And yet, in reality, I have not written this book alone. It reflects the thinking and learning I have received from many of my colleagues and friends, and the love and support from all kinds of important people in my life.

I would like to praise publicly:

Paul Hersey and *Spencer Johnson* for their genius and creativity. I had the privilege of co-creating Situational Leadership® with Paul and The One Minute Manager® with Spencer. Both of these experiences changed my life and the way I thought about managing and teaching people.

Norman Vincent Peale, my friend and spiritual guide, for helping me to take positive thinking everywhere in my life, even on the golf course, and for our writing experience together, which greatly influenced this book.

Jerry Tarde, editor of *Golf Digest*, and *Bob Toski*, golf teacher, player, and writer extraordinaire, for motivating me to find the connections between golf and management.

Chuck Hogan for opening my eyes to the mental and self-management sides of golf, and to *Kerry Graham* and *Lynn Marriott* for showing me how to put these to work on the golf course.

Tom Crum and *Tony Robbins* for their friendship and continual push for all of us to be the best that we can be. Their thinking has been important in this book.

Chihiro Isa, my Japanese translator and friend, for pressuring me to finish this book.

Joan Shedd, the Golf University office manager, and our teaching staff *Kathy Dougherty, Dave Emerick, Dean Lind, Lynn Marriott, Tom Wischmeyer*, and *David Witt*, for their help and support in writing this book and for making the Golf University a great organization.

The 2,500 or more golfers who have attended our Golf University over the last four years for their willingness to learn our approach to the game and give us enthusiastic feedback.

My longtime friend *George Malti* for all his help and support with the Golf University, his tremendous feedback on this book, and all the wonderful times we have had playing golf together around the world.

Jay Sigel for his inspiration as a golfer and friend, and for his help on this book.

All my golfing buddies and managerial friends who read drafts of *Playing the Great Game of Golf* for their helpful feedback.

Larry Hughes for his publishing vision and the fun we have had playing golf together, *Larry Norton*, head of Sales at William Morrow, for his feedback and encouragement on this book, *Will Schwalbe*, my editor, for making it a better book, and *Margret McBride*, my literary agent, for always being there for encouragement, advice, and a good laugh.

Bob Nelson, our Vice President for Product Development at Blanchard Training and Development and writing cohort, for his usual editorial excellence and frank and helpful feedback.

Eleanor Terndrup for not only typing *Playing the Great Game of Golf*, but embracing every word with love and care no matter how many times I made changes. I don't know what I would do without her.

My wife, *Margie*, who has put up with my addiction to golf for years and is now even getting hooked herself.

My daughter *Debbie*, a rapidly developing golfer, for enduring my storytelling about her in speeches and seminars over the years, and now in this book.

My son *Scott*, who went from a beginner to scratch golfer in four years, for making things happen at the Golf University as general manager, and for being one of the people with whom I enjoy playing the most.

And finally, my dad for introducing me to the great game of golf and my mom for making sure I got to play as much as possible when I was young. Those early years solidified my love for this game.

SERVICES AVAILABLE

The Golf University in San Diego, California, co-founded by Ken Blanchard, offers cutting-edge golf programs designed to help you break through to lower golf scores, more enjoyment of the game of golf, and an increased knowledge of leadership and team building.

In golf, the university has three regular courses available in two-, three-, and four-day formats to take you from start (the practice range) to finish (the golf course) with the great game of golf: G.U. 101, *The Short Game School*, emphasizing play from inside fifty yards; G.U. 201, *The Full Game School*, teaching all the mechanical, mental, and physical fundamentals of golf; and G.U. 301, *The Playing School*, focusing on mental preparation and self-management on the course. *Playing the Great Game of Golf* is the text for this course.

Two specialties of the Golf University are *Adventure in Golf*, a program for women only, and our *Team Building and Golf* programs. Adventure in Golf is taught by two of the country's finest LPGA professionals and has been specially designed to welcome women into golf by providing them with all the on-course and off-course knowledge they need to enjoy the great game.

Rather than being put in situations where they have to overcome fear for their life, our Team-Building and Golf Program participants have to overcome the same fears they experience every day at work: fear of failure, fear of disapproval or criticism, fear of losing control, fear of not pulling their own "weight," and the like. This program teaches leadership and team building concepts in the classroom and then uses team play on the golf course to apply learnings.

Special programs in Team-Building and Golf can be designed as the golf outing portion of regular business conferences or conventions, or as separate one-, two-, or three-day programs.

The Golf University is headquartered at the Mobil 4-star Rancho Bernardo Inn in San Diego. Our campus is unmatched for facilities and services, including ninety holes of challenging golf, a superbly equipped health club and spa, and award-winning restaurants.

For further information about the Golf University, write to: 17550 Bernardo Oaks Drive, San Diego, California 92128, or call 800-426-0966 or 619-485-8880.